KING'S HORSES

SAVAGE FALL DUET BOOK 2

LANA SKY

King's Horses

ACKNOWLEDGMENTS

Erica and Mickey, thank you so very much for taking the time to help me perfect this draft. As always, your feedback and expertise have been invaluable. Thanks to Melissa Stevens for such beautiful covers. Thank you, Charity for applying the final touches on this draft, and the many beta readers who provided encouragement along the way.

This story is a dark, twisted romance that contains subject matter that may not be appropriate for some readers including mentions of sexual abuse, child abuse, violence, and mentions of eating disorders.

PROLOGUE

BLAKE

NUMBERS. That's all these corporate bastards give a damn about. Shares, figures, dividends—goddamn numbers.

How they stack up.

How they fall apart.

Their investments are a house of cards, ripe for one bad shake to send it all crashing down. They make it too easy in the end. Disrupting the entire game with the stroke of a pen is almost child's play.

And with four new companies under my belt this week alone, I've bought the entire goddamn game board.

Even so…

I'm still running out of fucking time.

"Gentlemen." Looking up, I face the four men dispersed around the round table. Some of them scowl while the others sport stoic expressions—for good reason. Unlike them, I'm not clinging to the prestige a few shares can buy me.

The entire company is in the palm of my hand.

And they fucking know it.

"Don't begrudge my shares too much," I say, my mouth quirked, "think of me as merely a new investor, under your wing. After all, I don't intend to impose myself."

Not yet, anyway. When all is said and done, I'll burn this fucking corporation to the ground.

I don't have a choice. Even if *she* gets caught in the middle of the blaze.

Snow. My jaw clenches as the boardroom fades. I can still see her: bloodshot eyes, pale skin. Fiery red hair. Still so beautiful. *Fuck.*

My fingers curl into fists, crushing her memory into the depths of my psyche—where she belongs. But, like always, she claws her way back to the forefront of my thoughts, haunting me. Always.

In retrospect, she was never meant to get caught in the middle. I had it all planned down to the last detail. Takeover the company and then crush it, liquidating its shares—I just didn't expect her to fight me for it.

Though, to be fair I shouldn't have been so fucking surprised. For years, I've heard rumors of the lengths the Hollings have sunk to. 'Favors' the eldest son would grant to someone he wished to manipulate. Hunter would gladly suck cock to climb up the corporate ladder.

But never her. Not Snowy. She was always my naive, selfish, spiteful fool—but never desperate.

Until now.

That frail little creature's all grown up. These days there isn't an ounce of fat on her body but the loss puts her bone structure in sharp contrast. The last time I saw her, she looked more like her mother than ever. Haughty. Spoiled. But even underneath the polish and shine lurks hints of the girl she used to be.

Her hair is just as red.

Her face just as round.

Her lips just as pink.

Snowy Gale Hollings, the girl I once loved more than life itself…

And now, knowing her deception was based on a stupid, childish fantasy?

I shouldn't feel a damn thing.

"Mr. Lorenz?" I grit my teeth and fixate my attention on the man across from me. "Frankly, if you don't mean to impose yourself, then I have to ask. What is the point of this?"

He gestures around him at my impromptu board meeting.

"My plans mirror yours, gentleman," I insist, employing the suave tone that my so-called father did best. Prevent any ounce of emotion from seeping into your voice. Never smile too hard. Blink at random intervals. Harrison Lloyd—the bastard had deception down to an artform.

"It's Blake, is it?" The man directly across from me cocks his head. His hands are braced against the table's polished wood, displaying the gold watch on his wrist and the signet ring on his left hand. He smiles in that way only men like him can. As though everyone with less than a million to his name isn't worth the time on his diamond-studded clock face. "Frankly, I won't question how you happened upon this newest company," he says, staring down his hooked nose. "But now that you have other enterprises under your belt, my associates and I will gladly buy you out of the Hollings shares."

"I think I'll hold onto my seat for now," I reply, matching his smirk—another trick Harrison taught me. Like wild animals, these men communicate in nonverbal cues more than speech. They piss on their holdings and snarl at interlopers, no better than a mangy mutt.

And like any feral beast, they require an alpha's bite to bring them to heel.

"And while my percentage of shares allots me not only a seat at the table, but a right to demand a vote on the chairman, I'll refrain from that choice. For now. Let me cut to the chase. I know you're all aware of the donation I'd like to make in the corporation's name," I say, changing the subject.

"Donation," one of the men retorts. "You mean the very generous *bribe* you've promised to that cuck Antonio Sebastián? I hear he already found another sap to parade around that gala of his. My vote is a no. I say we focus on other matters."

"Oh," I say, nodding. "You mistook me. I'm merely *informing* the board. I'm not asking for permission."

The man sputters, redness blossoming over his hollow cheeks. "Y-You—"

"Enough." One of the men seated beside him scoffs. "Get a hold of yourself, Ramsey," he mutters before turning to me and extending his hand. "Welcome to the board, Blake. I trust you'll fit right in. Only the shrewdest of backstabbing cucks could manage to claim a majority of Hollings shares overnight."

His laugh suggests his words are in jest. But I know that look glinting in his dark eyes. It takes a backstabbing cuck to know a backstabbing cuck.

"I prefer Lorenz," I tell him while shaking his hand. "Blake Lorenz."

"Ah…" His eyes narrow, intensifying their stealthy scrutiny. "You wouldn't happen to be of the Frankfurt Lorenz's?"

"That's the one." I force a cold smile. "My father would be pleased to know that his humble reputation has reached all the way to the States."

"Humble?" The man guffaws so hard he damn near falls off his chair. "Given the way your family has overtaken Europe I'm not surprised Hollings enterprises were your next conquest."

He's equal parts impressed and alarmed. As he should be.

"But there is the question of that messy merger situation back in your country. What's the company again?" He pretends to mull it over, but his eyes are too sharp for true ignorance. "H.E.T.Z Corp? Run by Hanz Zipler, I think? Now *there* is a ruthless son of a bitch. Wasn't he married to your—"

"Are we bringing gossip to the boardroom now?" I ask, raising an eyebrow.

"N-No." The man's cheeks redden, but like a dog with a bone, he digs in. "Though Zipler, he had a big share of your family's company, didn't he? Nearly half."

I flash a smile that makes the bastard gulp. "In my experience, a businessman's fortunes can change at the snap of an even more ruthless man's fingers."

And Zipler's is already between my thumb and fucking forefinger. Case and point: we're at the top of the Hollings building. *My* building. The entire world is exposed below from beyond floor-to-ceiling windows. Everything from the waterlogged harbor to the endless jungle of skyscrapers clawing at the sky. The entire world: that's how people like the Hollings view this lone city. Any other destination is a mere detour, a pretty spot on the map. This place is where their heart lies; the proverbial nest of the snake.

"I thought it was time to try my hand at entering the American markets." I deliberately copy the man's callous tone.

He nods. "I can see that. Jacob Marshall, at your service."

The other men take turns introducing themselves not that I give a damn to remember them all. They sit at this table, in these chairs and dare to look at me like an outsider.

While they dallied in corporate offices, I cut my milk teeth on the walls of this building. Harrison Lloyd may not have been my biological father, but his blood, sweat and tears formed its very foundation. The layout may have changed and the furniture more modern, but at its core this entire fucking complex is the same.

Minus the name: I bet that motherfucker couldn't wait to drop the Lloyd surname from it.

"Blake?"

I flinch at the voice. It's not Emily's, my usual assistant. *Fuck.* Lurching forward, I hone my gaze on the figure at the door and bite down a curse.

Sure enough, Masha has her head stuck through a small crack in the door, her cheeks flushed pink. The other men watch on, barely concealing their amusement and curiosity. I catch one of them eyeing her bare legs and I have to remind myself of one thing: still need his signature. *Can't kill him.*

"What is it?" I demand, fighting to keep my tone level.

She lowers her head contritely, her voice so faint I have to strain to hear her, "I need to speak with you."

"Oh." Any irritation I felt instantly dies. Masha knows better than to interrupt me for anything other than matters concerning two people.

The first has avoided me for two damn months, ignoring every call and letter sent her way.

And the second…

"Well gentlemen," I say, flexing my fingers against the table, hard enough so each knuckle cracks, "I think we should cut this meeting short. I'll be expecting your approval of the donation however."

A second's pause gives any fucker the chance to argue.

No one does.

Standing, I lead the way to the door as they scramble behind me. Masha is the only one who follows me wordlessly into my office across the hall.

"What is it?" I ask, approaching the large oak desk dominating the center of the room.

Facing me, she lowers her gaze, her lips pursed. She's practically swimming in the dress I bought her, wringing her hands nervously over the navy, businesslike frock. With her blond hair scraped into a bun and little makeup, the average onlooker might peg her at sixteen—at the most. Not nearly twenty-one.

Her lips tremble, fighting to coax out words, but she doesn't even have to fucking say it.

"He contacted you again." My hands curl into fists and the closest victim is the wall. *Bang!* My knuckles sear as they meet the polished wood. Once. Twice. Again. Blood streaks my fingers when I finally unclench them. "That son of a bitch—"

"He wants me back," she says, almost in a whisper. Her tormentor needs no introduction. Only one bastard can make her sound this hollow. This empty. "He said... Blake, he'd forgive the debt if I come back."

"That same old lie," I remind her. "And I told you. I would handle it."

"You shouldn't have to!" Her voice is too flat to hold any real emotion so she raises her shaking hands instead. Unsteady, they claw at her neatly arranged hair, ripping strands from the coif. "This isn't your fault."

"Enough!" Irritation makes my tone harsher than I intend. "He was *my* goddamn father too."

The original Blake Lorenz: a man I barely knew, who both saved my life and shackled me to his in the same fell swoop. As a Lorenz, I'm freed from the taint of the Lloyd name.

But my real father had his own demons—a crushing load of silent debt so vast it was basically a death sentence. A burden he gladly shouldered, right to the grave. Anything to save his only daughter.

I could only hope to match his selfless devotion.

But I don't plan on dying anytime soon.

"No," I hiss, meeting Masha's gaze directly. "You're not going back to him. I already have Hollings enterprises and this week alone we've incorporated four smaller corporations."

"But it isn't enough," she says, shrugging her thin shoulders. "Unless you consume every company in the whole city it will never be enough."

"I told you not to worry yourself about that. You leave the business to me." Gritting my teeth, I add, "Want me to make it easier? You don't have a choice—"

"Don't I?" She's jutting her chin into the air, her jaw tight. "You've already lost so much because of me."

"Lost?" I nod to the windows and survey the view, shutting out the grim reality for a thundering heartbeat. The world of the Hollingses lies outstretched before me, kissed by the pinkish glow of mid-morning. "It looks like we've gained to me," I say. "You need a city? I'll buy this one, and then another. However many it fucking takes."

"And what about Snowy Hollings?"

Her name is like a fucking switch. One flick of it and my entire perspective on the world changes. For the worse—power is a simple goal, easily obtained.

But Snow? What I want from her can't be granted via a simple board meeting. Or with money, apparently, considering that in two months she has yet to accept the amount I offered her.

Suddenly drained, I collapse into the leather chair behind my desk. There's a stack of envelopes lying there, along with messy piles of paper.

The irony is a bitter pill to swallow. Once, she claimed to have given me her truth through her letters.

And I can't write a single goddamn one to explain mine. "Don't mention her," I finally muster the energy to reply. "Don't—"

"What happened to her family... It's my fault. You did that because of me—"

"No." I turn to my desk and swipe my hand over the surface, knocking everything on it to the floor. "It was never about you."

Always her. Beautiful, fiery princess Snow. Once, before Masha, I would have given her the world. I promised it to her.

"One day I'm going to live in the heart of Mayfield," she used to boast. "Right in the center! And I'd want a throne, of course. Red, placed perfectly to take in my servants."

"Stop worrying." I banish Snow with a shake of my head and stand. Masha trembles when I cross over to her, wrapping her in my arms. Mouth against her hair, I swear, "I won't ever let him hurt you again. Ever—"

"It would be easier if you sent me back," she insists, her face buried against my chest. "It would."

"But I won't," I say, gripping her tighter. "Don't even think about it."

"Just promise me one thing." Her small hands find mine and pry them from her waist, intertwining our fingers. "Just one thing."

I nod. "Anything."

"Promise me you won't hurt her again. Snowy. Please—"

"I promise." A part of me twinges, knowing deep down that it's a lie.

Snow can run for now. Hide away. Ignore me.

But her company was just the start. Child's play.

She was always the real prize—and some way, some goddamn how I'll make her see reason. I'll get her back, as easily as another fucking business.

Only this time, I won't ever let her go.

ONE

SNOWY

A FLAWLESS VENEER can make anything seem shiny and new again. All it takes is the perfect shade of red lipstick and a smile. But buyer beware: One peek beneath the hood betrays the sad truth.

The poor thing isn't even worth owning for free.

"You look beautiful, Snowy," Ronan insists. He started using this soothing, careful tone after my discharge from the hospital nearly eight weeks ago. "Beautiful. But if you don't want to come, you don't have to."

"I'm fine," I croak, forcing a smile. "Besides, it's just the Sebastiáns' benefit gala. We've gone a million times." Damn. My voice cracks despite my best efforts, and Ronan's grimace conveys what I can't say out loud.

Sure, our family has regularly attended the annual gala— but never once have we arrived penniless and scandalized.

"It's okay if you aren't ready. You don't have to listen to Hunter," he adds partially beneath his breath. "I can handle him."

Oh, Hunter. As he liked to reiterate, we Hollingses have attended the Sebastiáns' annual benefit gala every year since the dawn of time. To avoid doing so now would raise more suspicion than we could weather. After all, paupers must choose their battles wisely.

"It's not just him," I reply softly.

"Forget the rumors," Ronan hisses without looking at me. "The tabloids print whatever crap they can make up to sell papers. But if you insist... I think you look beautiful."

I bite my lip to smother a groan. He means well—I know he does. But the woman in my reflection isn't beautiful by any standards. Her pale skin hides a sickly hue, tainted by secrets she can't reveal. A vicious scar claims the right half of her face, reddened and scabbed, but her eyes draw the most concern: They're empty—despite how wide she makes her smile.

King's men, Snow, a cruel voice reminds me as I rummage through the makeup scattered on my vanity. A dash of pale lipstick doesn't banish dread. *Don't you see? Nothing can put you together again.*

"I'm fine," I insist without taking my eyes from the mirror. *Am I trying to convince Ronan or myself?* "Besides...it's been ages since I've seen Sloane."

"She tried calling you earlier," Ronan remarks, a polite way of phrasing: *she's tried contacting you for weeks.* "If you're not ready to go out, maybe we should—"

"I'm fine," I repeat for the umpteenth time.

"Good. But… Are you sure about *this*?" He fingers the collar of my modest black cocktail dress and my shoulders slump in defeat.

He has a point. The long-sleeve garment resembles something better worn at a funeral. My hair doesn't help matters any, slicked back into a bun as tight as its short length allows. The look is a far cry from the colorful couture creations I'm known for wearing, and the contrast doesn't escape me.

As shallow and stupid as I was just a few months ago, at least I had something then that I lack now. *Hope* sounds far too dramatic a term to describe it. Maybe it's naïveté, I used to be so fucking *naïve.*

Pretty dresses and lovely colors can't disguise the terrible lies drilled into me since birth. Someone clawed them out into the open, and the truth has finally seeped through the cracks.

Two months free from the hospital and I feel no less broken.

Not that I can say any of this to Ronan. Not the truth about my parentage or the real culprit of the man who assaulted me all those years ago. At least when it comes to Hunter, I only need to smile. Like a true Hollings, he'd rather focus his attention on reassembling our broken kingdom than waste time trying to fix me.

"Are you ready?" As if on cue, my other brother sticks his head through my bedroom doorway. He's the ivory contrast to Ronan, wearing a tux in a light shade of gray.

"Yes," I say, contorting my lips to match his grin. "In just a minute."

"Good. You look…nice."

I don't miss the look he and Ronan share before he retreats down the hall, and I watch him go, fingering the hem of my dress. "Maybe I should change?"

Ronan quickly averts his gaze. "You know what, Snowy? How about I get you something to eat before we leave? Give me five minutes." He practically runs off, leaving me trapped before my vanity and alone with the stranger staring back at me.

My brothers aren't the most nurturing of siblings, but *this* hurts the worst of all: the blatant ignoring of the elephant in the room. The way they both look at me as though they're afraid I'll crack at any minute. To prolong the inevitable, they dance on eggshells.

And I'm so tired of the fucking charade.

Then do something about it, a part of me hisses. Frustrated, I push back from my vanity table and turn to the small pile of clothing I left on the bed.

This room is on the top floor of one of Mayfield's premier hotels, decorated to excess. The view beyond my window is enough to command a steep price point—and deep down, I know we can't afford a single night, given our current finances. How Hunter and Ronan managed to avoid having us thrown onto the street, I've yet to discover.

I don't want to.

Maybe the stress of worrying about such matters is why they focus so much of their attention on me? Ronan himself purchased these dresses, paying for them only God knows how. I finger one: a flashy red cocktail dress from my favorite designer's private line. The strip of silk probably cost more than a week in this penthouse suite, and he offered it to me like a paramedic administering a last-ditch dose of adrenaline.

Sighing, I strip my black dress and slip the red one over my head. God, it barely even fits. The neckline gapes over my flat chest and flares out at my waist. Ronan must have gotten a larger size. To drill it in?

Without long sleeves to hide behind, the grotesque creature I've become eyes me warily from the mirror. *He's won, Snow,* she tells me. *Just admit it already.*

And maybe he has.

My hands shake, pawing at the flared skirt as if trying to find my old self lurking in the threads. All I find is loose bits of satin and, as a last resort I fish a pair of socks from a chest of drawers, recalling an old cleavage trick of Sloane's.

Three socks stuffed into each bra cup add some lift to the front of the gown. My hair I leave loose around my shoulders, salvaged by a gold headband. Repeated washes have rinsed out most of the dark-brown dye that had stained it, leaving the once fiery curls a rust-colored hue. A swipe of red lipstick along my mouth makes me look somewhat human again at least.

Maybe I'm not beyond repair just yet...

"Wow!" Ronan exclaims when he returns and finds me adjusting the final touches to my improved ensemble. His mouth cracks into a real smile as he places a plate of crackers on my vanity. "You look amazing, Snowy."

He's still lying. But this time, if I squint, I almost believe him.

"Thank you." I march over to him and take a bite of a cracker without being prompted. Once I've mechanically devoured three more crackers, he extends his arm.

"Shall we?"

Together, we meet Hunter in the foyer, and he does an exaggerated double take of my new appearance.

"Dazzling, Snowy," he says before grabbing my hand to give me a spin. He's a better charmer than Ronan, but his eyes always give him away. It's not my dress he's observing, but my legs, and my arms, and my hips.

Because, without anything to hide behind, there's no escaping the awful truth: I'm a shadow of who I used to be.

Something in my facial expression must change, because suddenly, both brothers stiffen, their smiles even more forced. "You look beautiful," they chirp in unison.

I let them rattle off more hollow compliments and bundle me in my coat before I exit the suite, one man on either arm. Tension taints the air, even if they don't want me to sense it. After two months, there's a reason they're dragging me out tonight, of all nights.

Not even trauma can keep a Hollings from the pursuit of money and power. We're off to see the wizard, with the hopes of making our fortune back—and I'm the last shiny trophy they have left to auction off to the highest bidder.

Considering that my ex-fiancé, Daniel Ellingston, was not only disgraced but fell off the face of the Earth, Snowy Hollings is open to a new master. Let the bids start at zero.

It isn't like they tell me as much, though they don't have to. Ronan keeps stroking my hair while Hunter makes sure to stand by my side, keeping me in plain view, lest we pass a rich, old baron on our way to the car. Who can blame them? I sure can't. We've performed the same song and dance for so long, I don't think they even realize how it makes me feel.

Worthless. Like one remaining sliver of the Hollings Estate yet to be burned to the ground.

"Are you sure about this?" Ronan asks while helping me into the back of a cab. But I'm not the one he's looking at. He and Hunter are communicating nonverbally again, trading loaded glances above my head like I'm not even here. "Maybe it's too soon—"

Hunter and I reply in unison.

"She's fine."

"I'm fine—*seriously*." I disentangle my arms from them both and enter the cab alone.

Something in the atmosphere changes, so potent that I can taste it: nerves. They sizzle from Ronan, obvious in how he keeps tugging at his cufflinks. Hunter fares no better, scowling out the window.

If I smile wider, perhaps he'll stop reaching for my hand every five minutes? I lift my lips at the corners only to feel his palm rasp over mine regardless.

"I can't wait to see Sloane," I say, forcing enthusiasm. "It will be nice to chat with her again. I'm sure she'll have all the usual suspects in attendance."

"Maybe," Ronan mutters, frowning. "But I want you to stay close tonight."

Irritation flares, making me clench my teeth. "Why?"

"No reason," Hunter says smoothly, beating Ronan to the punch. "We both want you to have fun tonight."

"Fun?" Ronan all but growls. Suddenly, he sighs and crosses his arms over his chest. "Damn it. Snowy, there's something you should know—"

"We're here," Hunter interjects while adjusting his tie.

Sure enough, the cab pulls onto the circular driveway of the Sebastiáns' breathtaking Italian-style villa. Towering at four stories and sprawled over countless acres, it's the bohemian counterpart to our family's once-traditional estate.

My throat tightens as I envision Hollings Manor. I haven't seen the property since the fire, but I have no trouble imagining the destruction: heaps of twisted wood and ash. Do I wish it were still standing? Weeks later, I'm unsure of the answer. So much hell lurked within its beautiful walls and gilded fixtures. Maybe it's better off burned to memory.

"Snowy?" Still tugging at the collar of his tux, Hunter exits the car first and holds out his free hand for me. The moment I take it, he clutches my fingers as if I'm a balloon in danger of drifting off. "Are you ready?"

He hauls me forward without waiting for a response. Ronan appears by my side, and between the two of them, I feel like a princess being shepherded to her doom by two executioners. Someone's signed my death warrant, but I won't know who until the very end of this charade.

There's no choice but to keep pretending until then.

Wearing our smiles like masks, we join the press of elegantly dressed guests ascending the curved staircase leading to the mansion's entrance. Up ahead, I can make out Sloane, who's greeting guests while dazzling in black silk. Something that could be regret pinches my rib cage, constricting my heart. I haven't seen her in so long. I'd almost forgotten just how charming she can seem when I don't have a fiancé for her to steal.

Speaking of which, how much of a spectacle do I make without my ring? My eyes trace the crowd with renewed interest only to find curious faces staring back. And no wonder. It strikes me now that this is my first time being seen in public since…

Since before I met Blake Lorenz.

Ronan mentioned the tabloids, but I know he's hidden the most salacious issues from me. Still, I gleaned the gist of them from articles I caught lying in crumpled balls around the suite. Hunter is a criminal. Ronan is a careless drunk, and I got the most dramatic title of all: recluse, suspected of a nervous breakdown over my family's demise.

"Snowy?" Hunter's grip tightens as he lowers his mouth to my ear. "What's wrong?"

"N-nothing," I croak, but I can't stop running my fingers through my hair. Its cropped length offers no protection from prying eyes.

One of the first things Ronan did when I left the hospital was hire a hairdresser to cut it to a proper bob—again, with no explanation of how he managed to pay for it. I don't even have enough curls left to disguise my healing scar.

Humpty Dumpty Snowy's irreparable cracks are visible for all to see.

"Shoulders back," Hunter mutters, and I balk, casting him a wary glance.

Papa used to say that very phrase, though admittedly harsher. "Shoulders back. Chin up. Remember who you are: a goddamn Hollings."

Rather than question his motives, I give Hunter the benefit of the doubt. Following his lead, I lift my chin into the air and hone my focus on the Sebastiáns' ornately carved entryway festooned with creeping vines. It's the only way I can keep moving.

When we finally reach the head of the procession, I hesitate. Inches from Sloane, I'm struck by the depth of my transformation. I used to be like her once. Smiling prettily while kissing wealthy billionaires on their cheeks and showcasing my enticing figure. So intent on her act, she doesn't even notice our approach until Hunter shakes her hand.

"Snowy?" Her brown eyes widen over my frame as her mouth forms a perfectly shaped O.

A heartbeat later, I find myself bombarded.

"Snowy!" Sloane exclaims while burying her face in my shoulder, muffling her musical accent. "I've missed you so much. Come. We have so much to catch up on."

She turns, dragging me toward the expansive foyer. I start to follow, but Ronan's grip on my opposite hand tightens. When I look back, he loosens his hold, but his worn smile only unnerves me further.

"It will be all right," he murmurs. "Just…stay close, okay?"

I nod, but I'm swept away by Sloane before I can question him. She steers me straight toward a gaggle of giggling socialites holding court near the back of her family's ballroom, and my brothers are instantly forgotten.

Unlike my family's stubbornly "old money" taste, the Sebastiáns relish in gaudier décor. Gold walls and white marble floors baste everything in a warm glow. A bit like hell. The moment I catch the first sly glance directed my way, another comparison comes to mind: fresh prey dragged into a lion's den.

Blood is in the air. Sloane does her best to give my hand a reassuring squeeze, but even she can't resist the promise of a spectacle. After my family's downfall and my sudden disappearance, I'm an easy target.

"Snowy!" One of the women we approach wrinkles her nose while casting me an appraising glance.

I recognize her instantly as Patsy Abernathy, my old high school tormentor, still blond and beautiful. Stunning in emerald couture, she poses with her left hand in full view— though it's hard to miss the giant rock sparkling on her finger regardless. The irony of it all almost draws a laugh from me. The last time I saw her, I publicly disinvited her from my wedding.

My, how the tides of fortune have changed.

"How wonderful to see you again," Patsy croons sweetly. She flicks a strand of blond hair from her face, allowing her ring to catch the light. Any more contorting and her poor hand will be one wrong move away from developing a stress fracture. "Such awful news about you and Daniel." She feigns a pout, her eyes gleaming mischievously. "I'm sure you have just the *best* tales to tell about your little getaway. Where did you go?"

The four women positioned around her lean in, watching me avidly to gauge my reaction. Even Sloane.

Dread washes over my skin. I find myself crossing my arms over my chest as if to guard the battered muscle within. *Where did I go?* I went into the Devil's private dwelling, where he crawled inside my head and tore my world to shreds. The worst part?

I allowed him to.

Tears prickle behind my eyes, but it's easier than expected to blink them back. Rage is a welcome antidote to pain. This blond bitch and her hellions have no idea what real agony is. I've crawled out of the flames of hellfire.

A trollop like her won't drag me back down.

My lips contort into an expression I haven't worn in so damn long. The nuances of it greet me like an old friend: a slow, stretching smile and slightly narrowed eyes. I meet Patsy's gaze head on and hold it until she blinks. The moment she does, I clasp her hand in mine.

"Oh, how attention-grabbing!" I exclaim as I brush my gaze over her ring. "A bit like old-fashioned costume jewelry. Not many people are brave enough to pull off that look."

A burst of nervous laughter erupts from the nearest guests. Good. Now to go in for the kill.

Still smiling, I step closer to Patsy and boldly sweep my hand along her shoulder. She shudders, another betrayal of weakness. Three months away from the Mayfield society scene and the tools for navigating it return like instinct. The way most people breathe without thinking, I manipulate. And intimidate. Papa taught me well, after all.

Garnering pity was always my chosen weapon, but not tonight.

"I wouldn't want to bore you about the nitty-gritty details of that mess with Daniel," I say, raising my voice so that it'll travel to every nosy onlooker pretending not to eavesdrop. "As for my family's current predicament, well, I'm so glad you're here. You know better than anyone what it's like to weather a scandal or two." Like one of her father's many public affairs—with women half our age, no less. "But anyway. Let's cut right to the chase."

As Patsy blinks in shock, I move in again, politely nudging her from the center of the conniving little group to claim the spotlight for myself.

"Enough about that," I declare, squaring my shoulders. "Who wants to learn all about my scar?"

TWO

THE LIES WERE ALMOST fun to spin, in retrospect. As far as Sloane and her cohorts are concerned, I spent the past four weeks in Tahiti, where I went scuba diving with a handsome instructor and injured my face learning to cliff dive into the sea. Sure, it's not the most engrossing of tales, but it did the trick.

It'll keep them guessing.

Just like that, Princess Snowy is back on her throne—but the thought doesn't comfort me the way it should. It feels far too easy to smile and schmooze with Mayfield's elite as if nothing ever happened to darken the Hollings's star.

Hell, tonight, I'm even graced with my own eclipse: Sloane's clinging to my side, murmuring all the gossip I missed over the weeks.

"...and then he gave her the money to fix the 'little' problem, of course," she stage-whispers as we pass a politician rumored to be in the midst of a scandal.

Suddenly, she grabs my arm. "Oh, and social climber alert. She's ruthless. Avoid her at all costs."

Her scorn is directed toward a beautiful woman with flowing, black hair, dressed in red. I don't recognize her, and at a glance, dressed in a modest gown, she doesn't trigger any alarm.

"Her name's Riley Haverty. A talk show host who runs some charity," Sloane explains while steering me along. "She's been hounding me for weeks, trying to get an audience with the illustrious Snowy Hollings—"

"A what?" I frown, giving the woman another glance. Caught between two wealthy men, she doesn't notice as Sloane smuggles me past.

"I told her to get in line," the Spanish beauty continues. "Like everyone else. If I have to hear someone ask me about you and Daniel one more damn time. Oh!" She lets me go and wiggles through two elegantly dressed women. "Papa's waving me over," she calls back. "I'll see you in a bit."

I have no choice but to press on without her. One must navigate the social order of Mayfield like a shark in the open sea; you stop swimming and you die.

Upon spotting my brothers on the periphery, I make my way toward them. At least Hunter could easily do all the acting for me; he's been so obsessed with our "reputation" lately. But when I try to meet his gaze, he's too busy chatting up a fellow guest to notice.

Unease spurs me on. Perhaps it's the glittery scenery, but this moment feels like glass. Fragile. It's as if some invisible clock is counting down the seconds until it's shattered. God, I can hear it beneath my heartbeat, steadily ticking away.

Three.

Two.

One.

"Can I have your attention, please?"

I turn, along with the rest of the crowd, to face the raised dais at the back of the ballroom, where Antonio Sebastián is standing before a microphone. His resemblance to Sloane is apparent in his sensual, shameless smile. A wealthy investor, he's a magnate in his own right, with sway almost comparable to what Father once commanded.

But even he can't afford to run such an event alone. The thought only comes to me now: With the Hollings money out of contention, which wealthy family rose to the occasion to claim the mantle of this year's star benefactor?

Given Patsy's gall to confront me, I'd stake my money on the Abernathys.

"I'd like to introduce the man of the hour," Mr. Sebastián begins as if reading my mind. "Without his generous donation, I'm sure the Children's Hospital wouldn't receive nearly the incredible support that we expect to give this quarter." He extends his hand beyond the crowd, toward a lone figure whose entrance must have been perfectly timed to coincide with his introduction. "Please join me in welcoming Mr. Blake Lorenz…"

Icy dread solidifies my limbs, rooting me to the floor. It's as if my entire body conspires to prevent me from turning around.

But it's too late. Driven by an impulse I can't name, our gazes connect, his one of chilling, unending blue.

Standing on the periphery, this mysterious benefactor gleams, a creature formed of shadow, illuminated by a spotlight that settles on him from above. He's dressed in the colors of destruction—a black tux and a blood-red tie— promising more with every step propelling him through a throng of gaping admirers.

Toward me.

I'm already turning on autopilot, pushing my way through anyone unlucky enough to be caught in my path. Shoving. Someone gasps and mutters a curse—I'm making a scene. Embarrassment sears my cheeks, but I can't stop. Not until I'm shrouded in the shadows of the ballroom. Then farther. Farther…

"Stop—"

He grabs my wrist from behind, halting me mid-sprint. Thrown off-balance, I stagger backward into a stone surface. A breathing, stiffening stone surface. We're in a hallway, one that branches toward the front of the house and is devoid of anyone else. When I step forward to escape, my captor grips me tighter.

"Just fucking wait a minute."

His tone sinks into me like a hook, spearing tender flesh. Caught, I'm spun around, forced to meet his gaze. God, it's like looking at a ghost. A demon. I find myself pinching the side of my hip—hard—to reinforce the painful truth.

This man isn't my Brandt. At least not anymore…

"Finally." He hesitates as he flicks his gaze over me, narrowed. "You look…"

I can guess the taunts he doesn't voice. You look broken, Snowy. You look disgusting.

I tug my arm, but his grip tightens.

"Wait."

In the glow of moonlight streaming in through a nearby window, I can only make out the stern line of his jaw, but there's no snarl distorting it. No glare lurks behind his gaze, either. Just shadow.

"We need to talk—"

"Why?" I'm not stupid. Hope is a weak fantasy I easily squash; I may have told him the truth, but in the grand scheme, it means nothing. Ten years of pain have done their damage, and no excuse on my part could ever make up for them. Weeks of reckoning with what happened between us on my own, however, still haven't prepared me for this. Seeing him. Smelling him. Hearing him: gruff but for once devoid of anger. Swallowing hard, I echo my pathetic question. "Why now?"

He flinches. Surprised? As if to compensate for that brief weakness, he steps in closer, towering above me. "You want a reason? How about business? My accountant is still waiting for a call from you."

I cringe, remembering his poisoned olive branch: a sum more than I could ever hope to recover from my family's finances—money we desperately need. And money I've left virtually in limbo, untouched.

"Are you waiting for an invitation?" he questions when I haven't answered. "After all this time, you owe me more than fucking silence, Snow."

Do I? I thought his parting gift in my hospital room was closure enough on his part—a birth certificate, in addition to the account transfer, confirming his identity. Yet the revelation just brought up even more unanswered questions. The foremost being: Why return now?

"What do you want from me?"

He levels his gaze against mine. "All I want is to talk."

"T-talk?" My mouth goes dry with the possibilities. Talk about how he destroyed my family home? My life? My brothers?

Months of silence and it seems fitting that he would choose now, of all times, to make his reappearance. If only to reinforce the truth he drilled into my skull: He'll never let me escape the past.

"I think you've said enough."

"Listen to me," he insists, reaching for my arm again. "Just let me explain. *Please*—"

"Snowy?"

The shout triggers alarm. *Ronan?*

Eyes flashing, Blake hisses, "Fuck, not now. Come with me." His fingers graze my forearm, but I'm already backing out of his reach. I can't let my brother see me like this.

Sensing my chance, I lunge, breaking into a sprint.

"Snow!"

Panting, I run through the dark, and footsteps echo, gaining on my position. Fast. Faster—too quickly to outrun.

"Snowy!"

Ronan. He's the one who grabs my forearm. My brain knows it, but my body reacts impulsively and I jump, wrenching away from him.

"Don't touch me!" I wrap my arms around myself, rubbing his touch away. Overly sensitive skin remembers everything I don't want to—every hateful caress. The cruel words snarled against my spine and whispered into my ear.

You're only beautiful like this, Snow. I'll only want you broken.

"Snowy?"

"I'm fine." My heart slams against my rib cage as fear mingles with guilt. I've never heard Ronan sound so worried. No, so *terrified*.

From behind him, I can see Hunter running, his hair mussed in haste. One look at me and he skids to a stop, his hands held before him.

"It's all right, Snowy," he says in that soothing, calm murmur only he can master. "It's okay. You're safe. We won't let him hurt—"

"I want to leave." God, I barely recognize the high-pitched voice tearing out of me. My hands are shaking. Wringing them together can't disguise the motion though. *I'm* shaking —and this time, I don't flinch when Ronan reaches for me, wrapping me in his arms.

"We are," he says. To Hunter, I hear him mutter, "We should have never brought her here. Fuck him. We'll just call the police the next time he sends another fucking—"

"Enough," Hunter snaps. "Now isn't the time."

I don't even try to follow the argument, as they steer me through the ballroom, past wide-eyed vultures desperate for a glance. He's watching as well—I sense him. Anger and cologne broadcast his location, so fucking close. Behind me? Numb, I can't even find the strength to look. I just eye the floor, clinging to my brothers as they forge a path through the crowd.

When we finally reach the cool night air, I realize I've been holding my breath all along. A bitter chill floods my lungs when I inhale, numbing me to my core.

"It's all right. We're leaving," Ronan insists while shoving me into the first town car that pulls up.

Sandwiched between him and Hunter, I struggle to catch my breath. To catch my senses. The only action my brain seems capable of has nothing to do with logic. Memories seep into the cracks where control has fractured. They taunt me with images, and feelings, and thoughts I've spent two months fighting to smother.

All the king's horses and all the king's men, Snow. No one can put you back together again. You're broken. Beautifully broken.

My brothers try to salvage the damaged pieces. They bundle me in their arms and rush me up to our suite. They ply me with promises of a bubble bath and a warm meal. The moment they leave to let me get undressed, I find myself staggering into the bathroom with the only goal of facing myself in the mirror.

Poor little Snowy Hollings. I was wrong to think wearing a stupid dress and lipstick could hide the damage visible on my skin. Angrily, I swipe the makeup off and sob openly at what I find underneath. A blind person could see it: I'm broken. Hollow. Ugly, selfish little Snow.

I'll always be that little girl who killed the boy she loved.

And he'll always haunt me.

Like a coward, I can't even run. So I cower over the toilet bowl, emptying myself of everything but pain. It's the only way I feel even an ounce of control.

Of something…

"Snowy!"

Oh no. I look up and find Ronan standing in the doorway, and I'd give anything in the world to avoid witnessing the pain lancing across his features.

All I can do is swipe my hand across my mouth, shaking with silent sobs. "I'm sorry," I croak, meaning every damn word. "Ronan, I'm so, so sorry."

THREE

"REMEMBER," the doctor says, standing before me in clinical white. "One session once a week. I look forward to meeting with you, Snowy."

My smile forced, I nod and then turn to the two men behind me. Wearing stoic expressions and gray suits, Ronan and Hunter resemble orderlies more than the disgraced businessmen they are.

"I'll get the car," Hunter explains before exiting the unit alone, leaving Ronan as my sole escort.

"Are you ready?" he asks, eyeing me warily.

I say nothing. Three days of inpatient psychiatric treatment and I'm right as rain. Honestly, I do feel better, even as my brother escorts me from the private, locked unit on the eighteenth floor of the city's most exclusive hospital.

All of those hours spent trapped here made one fact apparent: Blake Lorenz is the least of my problems.

Strange things have a habit of being revealed in family therapy sessions. Like the fact that Ronan and Hunter have been corresponding with a medical team for weeks, even before the night of the Sebastiáns' gala.

"We're worried about you, Snowy," Hunter had the nerve to insist, even while he surreptitiously eyed his cell phone beneath the unit's conference table—watching the stocks, I presume. "Lorenz did something to you," he added, his teeth bared. "If you just tell us what it fucking was, then we can nail the bastard—"

"Your well-being is all that matters," Ronan insisted, cutting him off.

Supposedly, that was their motive for turning their backs on me. Covert photographs of a skeletal stranger fill my medical record, along with secondhand descriptions of my behavior for the past eight weeks. I've lost five pounds, apparently. I've stopped eating. Stopped sleeping. As Ronan relayed to my therapist, he and Hunter were concerned.

Concerned enough to recommend an extended treatment facility outside of Mayfield against my protests. Concerned enough to offer an ultimatum: treatment, either voluntarily or otherwise.

Concerned enough to lie to me all this time.

I can process it all now with an almost detached sense of curiosity. After all, the joke's on me. I thought I'd been doing such a great job of coping. I smiled on cue and danced like a puppet on a string when asked. But the moment I falter on the world's stage? Oh, no. It's time to hide me away.

"Please say something," Ronan urges as he wrestles with a rolling suitcase containing my belongings and attempts to drag it onto the elevator leading to the hospital lobby. The wheels keep getting stuck just beyond the closing doors. Exasperated, he glances up and tries to shove the extended handle of the suitcase down into the body. "Give me a hand?"

I cut my gaze to the gleaming buttons on the elevator's interior, but I can't seem to move. Gradually, the doors meet, blocking off my view of a startled Ronan.

"Snowy!" He lunges a fraction too late.

Ding! The elevator's already descending, and seconds later, I arrive on the first level alone.

A good sister would wait for him to catch up. She certainly wouldn't merge into the stream of visitors with her head lowered to keep from drawing attention. She wouldn't slip down the first hallway she came across with no goal apart from…

What? Running?

Perhaps all I want is some fresh goddamn air. I'm so fucking sick of having my every moment scrutinized and maneuvered like a pawn on a chessboard. I'm so fucking *sick…*

Strangely, the anger I feel isn't even directed at Ronan or Hunter. Every ounce of rage festering inside me has only one target: myself.

"I was angry at the world," a woman says. The veracity of her words makes me freeze, mid-step.

At first glance, I see no one around, and dread gnaws at my nerves. Am I that desperate for validation that I hallucinated it? No. The voice is real, coming from somewhere nearby. A doorway, I realize.

Curious, I find myself drawn closer, peering into what looks like a lecture hall. At a podium stands a beautiful woman with cocoa skin and black hair hanging freely down her back. Dressed in a red pantsuit, she stuns almost as much as her heartfelt words. Her face seems familiar somehow, though I can't place it to a name.

"Do you want to know the worst part?" she asks the attentive crowd seated before her. "Everyone kept tiptoeing around me like I was some fragile porcelain doll. Like I'd cry at the drop of a hat. They thought I was 'depressed' or 'wallowing in despair,' but I wasn't." She shakes her head and hones her blazing, brown eyes on a distant spot, beyond the reach of those around her. "I was angry. And while I may have been raped, that didn't mean I was dead."

Raped. That word triggers alarm that has me scurrying back out into the hall. A bitter ache starts up in my stomach. Guilt? For the first time in so damn long, it feels as though someone is finally voicing what I can't say. How fitting that it only cements reality like a slap in the face: the elephant in the room. Despite how he treated me, Blake Lorenz *didn't* assault me. At least…I don't think I can call it that.

I stayed with him willingly. Even the sex was consensual. *And*, a twisted part of me adds, *you enjoyed it.*

I cringe away from the thought and then find myself leaning against the wall of a deserted hallway, panting. The longer I dawdle, the more elusive my freedom feels. Ronan's probably torn the whole hospital apart by now or called in the SWAT team. I almost feel bad for abandoning him. Almost.

But not too long ago, he abandoned me to be Hunter's babysitter, forced to cater to his fragile ego after our family's company went to ruin. I never consorted with doctors behind his back. I never betrayed him.

"Excuse me?"

Oh no. Soft footsteps approach, and I look up, fully prepared to find a security guard ready to escort me back to my brother. Instead, an amused pair of brown eyes takes me in, gleaming with genuine interest.

"Snowy Hollings," the woman says. "Don't tell me that the one time I stop contacting your family's offices is the one time I'm graced with a meeting?" Her warm laugh dispels any hostility the words may convey.

Regardless, I blink. "Excuse me?"

She's the woman from the podium, I realize. But wait. Even stranger, I think she's the same woman from the gala as well. The ruthless social climber, according to Sloane.

Up close, she radiates a steady confidence even Forrest Hollings would take note of. She tilts her head, eyeing me with a black eyebrow raised. "Or perhaps you were merely minding your own business and the fact you stumbled upon this meeting was entirely coincidence?"

I glance over her shoulder to find that I only managed to take a few steps from the lecture room she spoke in. Soft murmurs allude to the fact that someone else must have taken her place at the podium.

"Look, it doesn't matter. I'm Riley Haverty," she says, extending her hand.

I return the gesture, but she doesn't release my hand.

"I have to say that I've been trying to meet with you for... Well, it doesn't matter now. Can I have just a few minutes of your time?"

Minutes. I cast a wary glance down the hall, but I don't hear the stampede of armed forces on my trail just yet, and it seems Riley Haverty doesn't take no for an answer. Before I can respond, she steers me into the lecture hall, where a petite blonde is speaking to the crowd.

"They told me to just get over it," she says, her voice breaking, "but you can't just 'get over' something that affects you so deeply."

When she finishes, Riley claps the loudest. "I run Haven," she explains to me as the applause dies off. "We focus our outreach on assault victims, male and female, and I have to admit that I have been dying to meet you, Ms. Hollings."

A frown tugs at my mouth. "Why me?"

Riley shoots me a curious glance. "Well, to be frank, you were a witness in one of the most high-profile sexual assault cases in the entire country, accusing not only your longtime friend but the son of your father's business partner. In the years since, you've become a societal icon in your own right. If anyone could serve as a powerful voice to bring attention to Haven and our outreach, it's you."

My stomach sinks and I'm driven a step back. "I don't... I didn't—"

"I'm sorry," Riley says smoothly, her voice soft. "I didn't mean to intrude or bring up uncomfortable emotions. I tend to have what they call 'a blunt approach' in some circles." She laughs. "My only point is that you could be a powerful voice. I'd love for you to lend it to our cause, even for one event. We have a fundraiser at the convention center later this week, and it would be more than beneficial if you came to—"

"Snowy! Thank God."

Oh no. I turn as Ronan appears in the doorway, his hair wild, his eyes glazed with worry.

Heedless of the attention he's drawing, he races toward me and grabs my arm the moment he's close enough. "Don't you ever scare me like that again—"

"I'm sorry," I say over him, forcing a fake smile for Riley's benefit. "I wish I could but...I just... I'm not much of a speaker."

With a polite nod, Riley sidesteps Ronan and starts toward the front of the lecture hall. "I'm sorry to hear that," she says over her shoulder. "But if you change your mind, come to the convention center on Wednesday. I'd love to see you there."

"I—"

"Snowy, let's go." With the efficiency of a correctional officer, Ronan manually steers me to the doorway.

Before crossing the threshold, I wrench my arm from his grasp. People are staring—how shameless. Papa would roll over in his grave. I hope he is.

"I'm not a child," I snap before heading into the hallway alone.

Contrite, Ronan trails behind me, but his concern taints the air. I think I'm more startled by his behavior than angry. I've never seen him like this—not even when my weight reached its most dangerous lows. An irrational sense of dread warns me that something else must be feeding his guilt.

If so, an answer doesn't make itself known during the ride back to the hotel. Once we reach our suite, however, Ronan grabs my shoulder, rooting me to the floor.

"Please, Snowy." His voice rasps, breaking openly. "Please. I know you're angry, and I know you have every right to be," he adds when I try to break away. "You're pissed. Okay. Maybe the treatment center idea was too much. So punish *me*. Go on a wild tour of the strip clubs, or find a cabana boy to scandalize, if you must. Anything but hurt yourself. I can't…I can't take it."

"It's not your fault," I admit. "I just…"

"It's okay."

I'm in his arms before I know it, squeezed to the point of pain—not that he seems liable to let me go, even if I break. For a split second, I'm his sister again and not a fragile piece of porcelain. I'd suffer any bruise to make this moment last.

"We fucked up. I know we did. We should have done more, but it's like you won't even tell us what happened—"

"You don't have to apologize," I admit, hating myself for ever taking my anger out on him in the first place. "I'm sorry. I know I haven't been the easiest to be around lately."

"It's okay." He grips me tighter. "Just give me something to do—anything at all. Please."

Anything? "I want information on the Haven campaign," I blurt out. "And I want to make a sizeable donation in our name. *And*…I want to go to her event this week."

I'm not sure where the sudden change of heart comes from. Guilt? Or newfound shame? Showing my face for a cause bigger than myself is better than skulking around the suite, tormenting my brothers.

"The Haven campaign? *Riley Haverty's* Haven campaign?" Ronan draws back and eyes me, his mouth wrinkled. Rather than give him an answer, I wait until he nods. "Okay. Fine. Whatever you want. But—"

I stiffen in advance of his condition. "What?"

"You meet with your therapist as agreed. Once per week. Deal?"

I nod, my sigh resigned. "Deal."

"Then consider it done."

Just how would he find the money to make such a donation? I try not to care. For the first time in days, I feel some semblance of clarity. Normalcy? Hope?

Maybe Blake Lorenz didn't destroy all of me. Maybe there's some small piece of good left in Snowy Hollings. The least I can do is auction it off for a cause that deserves it.

FOUR

BLAKE

NEARLY A WEEK later and it's still all over the papers. Every tabloid, even the odd mainstream imprint, runs the same grainy photo. Her running, her head downcast, eyes so fucking wide.

Poor, pathetic Hollings girl. That moniker is her identity now, immortalized by the paparazzi in one brutal snapshot —but none of those casual spectators know the real truth behind her tormented expression.

Little Snow was fleeing from me.

She was terrified of *me*.

"Mr. Lorenz?" The intercom on the end of my desk buzzes, distorting the feminine voice coming through it. "You have a call on line one."

I reach out and strike a button on the console so hard the damn thing issues an alarming snap. "Thank you, Emily."

It's about fucking time.

The phone is in my hand before I even register grabbing it, cradling the receiver against my jaw. "Tell me you've done it."

"Damn," a woman replies, her tone crisp. A delicate laugh inserts a false sense of charm that only reinforces the warning I can sense from here. *Watch yourself, Lorenz.* "Perhaps next time answer with a greeting. Something to make me feel less like an awful, preying vulture than I already do—"

"I apologize," I reply smoothly. "Feel free to double my last donation. Satisfied?"

I wait.

She's silent.

"Now…" My fingers curl against the polished wood of the desk as I fish for the right phrasing. There's so many fucking things I need to say. Ask. Demand. In the end, I can only spit out, "is it done?"

"Well, I've met her if that's what you mean," she replies. I hear her inhale dejectedly. She must be alone, wallowing in her guilt.

"I'll triple my donation if you stop beating around the fucking bush." I yank the phone toward and stand, turning to the view below. The city sleeps, a maze of gray concrete and twisted metal. Somewhere amongst it all, Snow is hiding away. I'll let her—for now, but every mouse has to scurry out into the open sometime. "Did you get her to agree or not?"

"I got her to come if that's what you mean," she finally admits. "And trust that I feel disgusting enough to doubt that even your very generous *bribe* is worth this. Why her? I think the poor girl has been through enough—"

"You don't need to concern yourself with her," I say, forcing more suave politeness into my tone. These days I feel more like Harrison than ever. Always lying, always balanced at the edge of a precipice.

All over a Hollings. The man would have gladly given his soul for Elizabeth, his partner's wife.

But I've already died for Snowy once.

"Just tell me again that spiel you spun before," the woman demands. "I know it's a lie but I'd like to hear it anyway: you won't hurt her."

"I won't," I reply. "Add another zero to my donation if it helps you sleep at night. Just remember our agreement."

I hang up, slamming the receiver against the base. Energy surges through my blood, demanding I pace. Crack my knuckles. Anything but sit and fucking wait.

I've gone from clawing my way to the top, to sitting at the top of the fucking pile, always waiting.

"Mr. Lorenz?" Emily announces through the intercom.

"What?" I snap without thinking, still stuck on Snowy. She doesn't understand now, but I'll make her see. No. More than that... I'll make her come *running* to me.

"You told me to tell you when yesterday's reports came in," Emily says, unperturbed by my tone.

"Right." I boot up the computer on my desk and open the latest email in my inbox. A smug grin is already forming, tugging at the corner of my mouth. Four businesses in two months, not including Holling's INC.

It's a fucking impressive feat.

But not impressive enough. Within seconds of scanning the latest corporate holdings, my smile becomes a frown. "Son of a bitch!"

Where I've taken over four of Mayfield's minor corporations, a foreign investor somehow managed to snag six.

My eyes narrow over the name and I form a fist, slamming it against my knee.

Hanz Zipler.

"Mr. Lorenz?" Emily calls tentatively. "Sorry to intrude, but you have another call. Line 2."

My eyes narrow further as I snatch up the receiver, tearing myself from the reports. "This is Blake," I say gruffly.

"You were supposed to leave her alone." This speaker is a man, his words slurring together. He's drunk, I suspect.

Were I in his place, I would be as well. "All of this… You said you'd leave her alone—"

"And you said you'd stay in fucking Tahiti, or Bali, or wherever the fuck you've run off to," I remind him. "You worry about keeping your head down and scraping together what little pride you have left and leave Snowy Hollings to me."

I hang up and grit my teeth, biting down the rage that feels so fucking constant these days. It sustains me more than blood, it feels like. Hate and anger and everything I've held onto for so damn long.

I could swallow up the entire damn city and it still wouldn't be enough.

I could amass more money than God.

Rule the entire goddamn world.

But claim Snow again? Make her see reason…

Maybe only *that* would ever be enough.

Or fuck, it could just be the beginning of another twisted power play, well beyond my games with Zipler.

We used to play chess, her and I. She relished the complexities of kings and queens, while I enjoyed the classic appeal of it: power and war. Her tactic was to always go after my most powerful pieces, leaving me with only pawns.

And, still, I always won.

Not because I was a better player, she just couldn't stand to ever deliver the finishing blow.

"You show your hand too soon," I used to scold her. *"You play softer when you think I'll lose it all. You let your guard down, Snow. When you think I'm on the brink of destruction, you always back down. That only makes it easier to trap you in the end."*

If only the world were still as simple as those childish games. The donation to Antonio Sebastián would have made the impact it should have. Snowy would have *willingly* attended the gala and meeting her there would have resulted in a miraculous reunion. Happy fucking ending.

Not this. The look on her face made it clear—I'm still the monster of her story. Now more than ever, I'm determined to do whatever it takes to twist that perception. Turn the tide of the game. Then win.

There is no option other than checkmate.

* * *

SNOWY

THE CONVENTION CENTER is a sprawling complex in the heart of downtown Mayfield, and I spend almost as much time admiring the building as I do trying to talk myself out of entering it. Not because I'm afraid of being seen. I'm not. It's just that the Haven campaign is much more well-known than I would have believed.

Every news organization in the city must be here to cover this event. Cameramen and reporters scour the property, interviewing guests at random.

Damn. I let loose a resigned sigh as I haul myself from a cab. It will be nearly impossible to sneak in unnoticed. Poor Riley. The last thing she needs is a tabloid headline courtesy of Snowy Hollings, the unstable train wreck who made a spectacle of herself at the Sebastiáns' gala.

My brothers couldn't shield me from the rumors for very long. Sloane herself ensured I caught wind of them by forwarding me a text linking an article sensationalizing my sudden departure. *My father threatened to sue,* she'd prefaced the message with. One look at the headline and I sensed the narrative being spun.

DISGRACED HOLLINGS HEIRESS STORMS FROM GALA

God, I barely recognized myself in the grainy photo attached to the headline.

No wonder Hunter looked seconds from tethering me to a leash before I left today. How I'd convinced him to let me go to this event alone, I have no idea. Perhaps the promise of this exact kind of publicity is enough to soothe his nerves —after all, anything to redeem the Hollings name.

Regardless, I soldier onward while clutching my purse to my chest. I'll make this quick—no hysterics, no scandal. Ronan's earned that much of a compromise.

Within minutes, I find Riley Haverty in the largest auditorium, charming a sea of supporters. At a glance, it's apparent that I missed the memo: Everyone seems to be wearing some shade of crimson, and I assume it must be the campaign's signature hue. Suddenly self-conscious, I tug at my sleeves. I dressed conservatively today, wearing just a blouse and a demure skirt.

In contrast, Riley's confidence permeates every minor detail of the décor. Banners promoting sexual-assault awareness hang from the walls, and sneaking insecurity festers the more I inspect my surroundings. Nearly everyone conveys striking confidence.

"Snowy?"

I jump as a warm hand settles over my forearm.

"You made it!"

Dazed, I find myself drawn into a hug by Riley Haverty.

Wearing a blazing shade of crimson, she cuts a commanding figure. "I had a feeling you would. Tada!" She reaches into a leather handbag and withdraws a small square of plastic: a name tag.

I gape, stunned. "I...I can't—"

"And you don't have to," she insists, dragging me forward, deeper into the auditorium.

We draw notice with every step, and I recognize the flash of cameras in our wake. Whether I want it to or not, word of my arrival will spread, and I cringe at how my family's taint might soil such an event.

"I just wanted to present this to you in person. Here—" I reach into my bag for an envelope and press it into her hand. The crumpled thing is damp with my sweat. Ronan came through with his magic donation, though I'm not brave enough to see the amount for myself. "It's nowhere near what you deserve, but—"

"It's more than enough," Riley says warmly. "And you being here is even more appreciated than money."

"Really?"

She winks. "Immensely."

The way she speaks weaves a spell that instantly relieves some of my nerves. Her poise is infectious.

"Stay for a bit," she implores. "Here—" As we approach a table sporting brochures containing information about the Haven campaign, she lifts a stack and hands them to me. "Pass these out. Smile. Trust me—your presence alone goes a million miles."

It's only now that I read the tagline accompanying the branding for this event. **Featuring speakers: Riley Haverty, Chloe Pracile, Amy Harville, and Snowy Hollings.**

I wince. Suddenly, my fingers are shaking too badly to hold anything, and the brochures fall to the floor. "I didn't… I can't speak," I say, stumbling over the words. "I'm sorry if you thought—"

"Oh, damn." Sighing, Riley sinks to her knees and gathers the pamphlets. Then she looks up, biting her lower lip. "I jumped the gun again, didn't I?"

Am I angry? I don't know. My emotions feel too sluggish to reach my brain, as though they're trapped behind something solid. Eventually, I settle on a name for the feeling tearing through my veins. *Guilt.* Out of all of those women, I don't belong here.

"I should go—"

"Please don't." Riley imploringly clasps a hand over her chest. "Please. I... It's just, if you don't mind my pointing it out, you were assaulted by someone close to you," she says, her tone soft. "That's the open secret: Most assaults come from the people we trust the most. Friends. Neighbors. Parents—"

I wince, though Riley doesn't seem to notice.

She clasps one of my hands in both of her own. "I'm sorry if I overstepped. At least listen to a few of our keynotes. I'll apologize for the confusion myself, and I won't drag you on stage without your permission. I promise."

Before I can reply, the lights dim and another woman takes the stage, announcing the start of the event.

"Please," Riley mouths before taking off to the front. "I'll make it up to you."

I waver on the tips of my toes, eyeing the doorway to the auditorium. A part of me wants to leave, remembering Sloane's warning. Or maybe it's just cowardice; here, I'm forced to stand without my mask. I'm just Snowy, a spectator like so many others. Alone, I settle against the back wall and just watch.

The speakers range in ages from barely eighteen to twice as old. Their stories are harrowing, detailing horrific abuse that puts anything I've experienced to shame. As Riley mentioned, there is a disturbing theme: friends, brothers, sisters, fathers, mothers. The worst abuse seems to come from within, and I can't help but picture Papa. I think it's the first time I ever let myself put him in that dangerous context I've avoided for so long: abuser. Denial is a Hollings defining trait, and I've admittedly painted his memory in so many bright shades to make it easier to look back and not…

Scream?

Multiple women verbalize the same conflicting emotions in heartbreaking detail. At the same time, they speak bravely, without flinching from the trauma of their past, and an air of hope settles over the crowd by the time the final speaker delivers her message to thunderous applause. Riley takes the podium next, and as promised, she mentions my family's donation and apologizes profusely for the confusion regarding my speaking.

So I don't know why the hell I step forward, cutting her off midsentence.

"I… Um, it seems she would like to say a word after all," Riley says smoothly while inching back from the podium. "Everyone, please welcome Snowy Hollings."

The applause that follows draws heat to my cheeks. How unwarranted. I'm cheered only because of my name—*that* name. Hollings. A name tied to Forrest and the darkest, most twisted things festering in my soul. How ironic is it that the Hollings name can be coveted by someone fighting a crusade against sexual assault with no clue as to how hypocritical it is that I'm even here?

In a daze, I mount the stage anyway, and I face a crowd of people who should be sniggering. Laughing. Not waiting.

Not listening.

I don't belong here, but no one seems to know it. They sit patiently in the lingering silence as I clear my throat, desperate to find words. In the end, I stop trying, pretending, and acting. I open my mouth and simply speak.

"I don't belong here," I admit before licking my lips to find traction to keep talking. "I'm not...I'm not a victim—"

Applause erupts, and I stiffen, mortified. They misunderstood me, thinking I meant the statement as one of empowerment. If only I were that brave. But I'm not.

"I wish I could say something inspiring or incredible like everyone else," I add weakly. "But I can't. All I can say is... No one wants to label events in their life as t-trauma."

God, I hate that word, but there it is. Traumatic: an event that shatters the world as one knows it. Only now can I finally let myself use it. I inflicted trauma on Brandt Lloyd —and the man I'd grown up believing was my father inflicted similar damage upon me.

Someone in the audience coughs, drawing my attention, and I blink, remembering where I am.

After clearing my throat, I try again. "Why would we? You're a good daughter. Or a good friend. You're doing what you must. If someone hurts you, you deserve it b-because…" I break off, heat searing behind my eyes. God, not now. I blink rapidly, clenching the podium to the point of pain. Before I can run, I spot a familiar face in the crowd. Riley.

"Go on," she mouths, nodding encouragingly. For the first time in so damn long, someone wants me to speak out loud, and I'm finding that I can't resist the temptation, even if it stings.

"If someone hurts you, you think you deserve it. You believe it. Maybe it's true…but… You aren't responsible for someone else's pain. Your feelings matter as well. Your body matters. No one should be allowed to violate it just because they feel they own it."

My teeth clamp together over the last words as I marvel at their ferocity. Who are they directed at? Papa? Myself?

I don't know, and as the crowd responds with applause, I don't have to decipher them.

At least for now.

* * *

THE REST of the event passes in a strange, dazed blur. For most of it, I follow Riley, greeting visitors with my plastic, fake smile. Eventually, she disappears, leaving me alone to my own devices.

And all I can do is stare.

The speakers mingle with the crowd and trade stories with visitors. They offer sympathy and convey emotions in ways even Mayfield's most adept social manipulators never could. They're genuine, and I find myself swept up in the chaos, just as riveted as the average visitor. It isn't until I notice the sky darkening above the glass skylights that I realize just how long I've gone without stressing about Ronan or Hunter's vigilance or fighting my own thoughts.

Haven feels more like a feeling than a name, and I wish I could make it last forever. All too soon, guests begin to trickle one by one from the auditorium until just a handful remain. I find Riley greeting the last few stragglers, but when she sees me, she nearly barrels me over in another hug.

"You are amazing!" she exclaims against my shoulder before pulling away. "You are amazing. Not one, but two donations, both equally generous?"

"Two?" I shake my head, convinced I've misheard her.

"Yes," she insists. "Your associate delivered it by hand not too long ago." Something in my expression must convince her to elaborate. "A man. Tall."

I sigh. Has Hunter gotten in on the action, attempting to buy my trust back as well? Probably. He's certainly charming enough to inspire the flush creeping into Riley's cheeks.

"Dark hair," she adds as a falling sensation washes down my spine, leaving me lightheaded. "Young. Handsome... Snowy?"

"I'm fine," I whisper even as I clutch the edge of a table for balance.

She gently touches my shoulder. "Are you sure?"

No... The word won't leave my tongue, but Riley's already scurrying across the room.

"Let me get you a chair," she calls back.

Movement catches the corner of my eye as a hulking figure steps from the shadows the moment she's gone. Black stubble coats his chin, and bruises beneath his eyes reveal lingering exhaustion. From lack of sleep? Any concern I may feel is all but shattered by the coldness in his gaze.

I've never seen such a hard, frozen shade of blue.

I've never seen someone so furious.

"Don't run."

I'm not sure if I imagined the strained growl. Either way, I'm already racing for the main doors, weaving through the thinning crowd—but I'm not fast enough. Mere paces from freedom, my arm is seized in a grip of iron. One tug has me off-balance. Before I can get my bearings, I'm steered into a narrow room just outside the auditorium.

It's small. Dark. I faintly make out a table and chairs, which reveals it to be a conference room of some kind—an ironic prison for Blake Lorenz to trap me in now.

"Let me go." My breathless whisper lacks any conviction, but he releases me anyway. When my gaze darts to the door handle, however, he places his hand over it, blocking it from view.

"All I'm asking for is five damn minutes."

"For what?"

His eyes narrow into slits. He's wearing a dark suit, which bolsters his true intent: He's not here for an idle chat, but business. "Seriously, Snowy, let's not play this game."

I'm not faking my confusion. "W-what game?"

"I'm sure you know the one," he suggests, raising a black eyebrow. "It seems to always begin with you running from me."

I can't stop smoothing my hands over the front of my blouse, tucking every part of me away from his scrutiny. "Did I...offend you at the Sebastiáns' gala? If so, I'm sorry—"

"The gala?" He laughs coldly, shaking his head. "Don't play coy, Snowy." There's a hard note I can't miss in his voice. Almost a plea. *I'm trying my best. Don't ruin it.*

"Okay, then what do you want?" I demand cautiously. "You could call or send a message. You don't have to ambush me—"

"I don't?" He blinks. "Funny you'd say that, because I've been trying to 'call or send a message' every goddamn day for two months and you've yet to give me a single response."

I shake my head, alarmed by the dark expression crossing his features. "You're lying."

"Am I? It seems your brothers have taken their roles as your gatekeepers much more seriously than you've given them credit for."

"And they shouldn't?" A defensive lump forms at the base of my throat. Ronan and Hunter have been nearly insufferable lately, but it isn't like they don't have a reason to be. "Let's not forget the fact that you had them find me naked, wandering the woods alone after you burned down our house."

"I haven't." He doesn't even wince. It's as if his face is a siphon, designed to filter all emotion. He's so different from the boy he used to be that it blows my mind. Brandt would never be so callous. If anything, he'd sense the tears welling behind my eyes, and he'd already start wiping them away. *King's men, Snow,* he'd murmur to reassure me. *I'll always be there to pick up the pieces.*

"Fine," I say thickly. "Then I don't think we have anything to discuss—"

"Listen to me. I didn't come here to fight with you." The genuine note catches me off guard. "I came here to warn you. Tell your brothers that they accomplish nothing by sending the police to my goddamn office every morning. I'm not the one threatening you, though I think you have a damn good idea who is—"

"Threatening me?"

He scoffs, studying me with a flick of his gaze. "You know damn well what I mean."

"What are you talking about?"

"Damn." A frown distorts his cold expression. For a second, he almost looks human again. Pitying? "They haven't told you…"

I can't keep the exasperation from my tone. "Told me what?"

"You've gone and got a bounty put on your head, Snow," he declares. "A nasty one. What the hell were you thinking, messing with a man like Lyle Harlow?"

Oh God.

The name triggers a dark wealth of memories, both old and new. Lyle Harlow was my father's lackey, known for engaging in criminal enterprises. Though it isn't like I can judge Papa too much, considering that just a few months ago, I consorted with Harlow myself to find the whereabouts of one Blake Lorenz.

"I demand my payment in full, Little Hollings," he warned me then. Only I never sent a dime.

I don't have one to spare.

Suffice it to say that a man who'd murder a teenager isn't above targeting an heiress to avenge a slight. "They haven't told you," Blake accused. Just what do Ronan and Hunter know?

"Did you fucking hear what I said?"

"Y-yes." I turn away from him, crossing my arms to disguise how they're shaking. "But I don't know what you're talking about."

"Bullshit. You went to Harlow. How could you be so fucking stupid—"

"And what if I did?" My vision blurs, and warmth paints my cheeks before I can swipe at the tears with the back of my hand. "Why does it matter to you?"

"Don't."

Alarmed, I look up and find him balanced on the tips of his toes, his entire body tensed like a coil ready to spring. I can almost visualize the ropes of his control snapping, one by one—a twitching finger here, a pulsing vein there.

Pulling his upper lip from his teeth, he growls, "You may not trust me, but at least give me the benefit of the doubt, Snow. Don't you dare treat me like I'm a monster. Not again."

I don't mean to counter him. I don't. But something hot rises in me like bile, impossible to keep back. "You cut my hair. You locked me away. You told me awful, vile things. You destroyed everything I ever cared about. What else does that make you?"

"Fine," he says, his tone dangerously soft. "Then what does that make *you*?"

Any reply I could say dies in my throat. He's right. I helped create the person he's become.

"Maybe I'm even worse," I rasp, regaining my voice. "So blame me. Hate me. Just let me go." I start forward, but he doesn't budge. If anything, he seems to loom above, infinitely taller.

"You need to listen to me. Pay Harlow. You have more than enough money—"

"*Your* money," I reply more harshly than I meant to. The money he made by selling off my family's business shares while making me believe he would let me keep them. Blood money. "I don't want it."

"This isn't the time for fucking pride, Snowy!"

I stiffen as he grips my shoulders and forces me to meet his gaze.

"Do you understand how much danger you're in? Do you know what a man like Harlow would do? He'd make an example of you." His fingers shoot out to graze my cheek, inching toward my healing scar. "He'd hurt you worse than I ever could. Pay him with the goddamn money."

"Let…let me go."

He immediately withdraws his fingers, scowling at the tips —but his opposite hand stays, rooting me to the floor. "You're playing with fire."

He sounds too serious. Too stern. My racing heart wants me to read more into it than I should. There's something ominous in the set of his jaw. It's the same way he looked the day he promised me the Hollings Estate.

"You're lying," I whisper.

"Am I? Or perhaps I'm here to 'abuse' you further? Violate your body? Claim I own it? Admit it: Was all that directed at me?"

My face overheats as I recognize the words of my impromptu speech spit back in my face. When I say nothing, he barks out a callous laugh.

"Of course it was. That was a rousing presentation," he declares, mockingly clapping his hands. "But, even now, you still can't accuse *him* out loud, can you? Say his name, Snow. Admit who really hurt you."

Forrest Hollings. My lips flutter, but words won't come. Ten years of lying and I can't find the voice to speak the truth a second time, even to the one person who deserves it the most.

"I thought so," he hisses. "It's still easier to blame me, isn't it? No matter what righteous reasons you may have had. Fine. I want to hear it from your mouth. So say it. Say I raped you for a second time—"

"Stop."

"It's what you let them think, isn't it?" He cocks his head, his gaze honed with laser focus. "Say it. Use me as your goddamn scapegoat. Tell me I hurt you."

Rape? No. But I can't begin to classify the damage he's done to me in other ways.

"You *did* hurt me." That voice was a stranger's, so weak. So pathetic.

"Did I now, Snow?"

I shiver as his eyes flash a dangerous blue.

"Tell me how."

No. I turn away, but his fingers hook beneath my chin, wrenching my head around to face him.

"Tell me," he commands. "This time, there is no judge. No jury. Tell me how I hurt you. In detail, Snow."

"Stop it—"

"Say it."

"Y-you lied to me," I hear myself croak, sounding miles away. More tears spill down my cheeks without warning, hot and punishing. "You violated me. You made me feel… you made me feel like I was worthless."

"Good." He lets me go, leaving me to stagger for balance. "At least now you know what it fucking feels like. You want to die? Be my guest," he calls on his way to the door. "But if you want to play the role of traumatized victim, try a little harder. Perhaps more tears as you run gasping from the room next time?" He chuckles while rubbing his chin. "Such intrigue swirling around, ever since your little display at the Sebastiáns' gala. Bravo. You certainly had them all fooled. They're whispering about who I am to you. An ex-lover? Blackmailer? High society minds certainly have quite the imagination."

"I didn't even know you'd be there," I admit, my voice thick.

"Ahhh." He rubs his chin, mulling over a different explanation. "Your brothers sure love exploiting your flair for the dramatics. Hunter, I bet."

He laughs again, hollowly. Then he clenches his fist and slams it against the wall between us.

"I publicized that fucking donation," he growls as I jump. "The whole damn world knew I'd be there. Then you show up, after avoiding me for fucking weeks, and you… You act as though *you're* the goddamn one hurting." His voice breaks, betraying something raw and ugly festering underneath. Just as quickly, a cold smile banishes any hint of anger. "Enjoy the drama, Snow," he says while wrenching open the door. "I look forward to hearing all about how I raped you in the tabloids."

He leaves, slamming the door behind him so fiercely that it rattles on the hinges.

All I can do is struggle to remain standing.

FIVE

I SPEND the next three days locked inside my room with only my window to connect me to the outside world.

Surprisingly, my brothers haven't mentioned the treatment facility, and I can't bear to broach the topics Blake brought up. Would Hunter really be so manipulative as to bring me into the man's orbit, knowing I'd crumble?

The answer lurks at the pit of my stomach: He's a Hollings. A part of me doesn't want to go there. Perhaps my brothers are simply worried and the so-called threats against me explain their sudden eagerness to ship me away? I'm not brave enough to ask.

In a bitter compromise, we silently coexist. Mistrust festers, gathering in the air like water swelling behind a fragile dam.

Until it finally breaks.

I wake up smelling the first sign of danger: Ronan's cologne. He enters my room without warning, and when I startle

LANA SKY

upright, I find him standing by the window, glaring at the streets below.

"Ronan?"

He cuts his gaze in my direction, and I gasp out loud. His eyes glow red—they're so bloodshot.

"What's wrong?" The blood drains from my face. "Is Hunter—"

"Why didn't you say anything, Snowy?" He sounds rough, the way he does when he's been drinking. Or…crying? God, he has been. Drying tears glisten on his skin, and my heart throbs warily. "I would have done something. I…I'd have killed that son of a bitch!"

Oh no. Only a few men could earn this amount of scorn from him. "What are you talking about?"

"This!" He throws something onto my bed that I didn't notice him holding. Flat. Square. A newspaper.

The blazing headline makes me do a double take. Blood rushes from my skull and pools within my overworked heart. I can't breathe. All I can do is read.

CHILLING EXCHANGE REVEALED ON TAPE, screams the headline, followed by snippets of said recording. I see my name. Blake Lorenz's. A list of abstract quotes supposedly from a recording.

"You hurt me."

Numb, I grasp the paper, drawing it closer. Ink smears beneath my sweaty fingerprints the faster I read.

"You violated me… You made me feel like I was worthless."

"Good. At least now you know what it fucking feels like."

Among the sordid snippets, there's no mention of the gala or Lyle Harlow. Just carefully constructed phrases to make it seem like…

To make it seem like Blake Lorenz did more than just torment me.

"Oh…God…" I pinch myself, raking my nails over my skin. But I don't wake up. This is real. Drawing my knees to my chest doesn't contain my throbbing heart. It hammers through my rib cage, leaving me hollow.

"I look forward to reading about how I raped you in the tabloids."

"Are you listening to me?" Ronan is still watching me, his expression agonized. "I knew he hurt you," he says, hissing through clenched teeth. "Somehow, even if you wouldn't admit the details. But never… Why didn't you fucking say something?"

He's joined by Hunter before I can answer. Stern-faced, our older brother flanks the opposite end of my bed.

"The board's put the bastard on suspension," he says, though I'm not sure if he's talking to Ronan or me. "If public opinion trends the way it seems, he'll be gone for sure. He's ruined."

"I don't give a damn about the company!" Turning from Hunter, Ronan lunges for my hand, yanking me upright. "Come on."

I stagger to my feet as he drags me down the hall and throws the door to the suite open. Alarmed, I clutch at the doorway with both hands. "Where are we going?"

"To the hospital," he says, casting me an incredulous look. "Or the police station. Fuck, we have to do something—"

"No!" I wrench out of his grip and pace mindlessly. My fingers tear through my hair as I remember the damage done to it and by whom. He did hurt me, but never in a million years would I do something like this to retaliate.

Never.

"When were you ever alone with the bastard?" Ronan demands. "Is this why... God, we should have never taken you to that fucking event!"

"Ronan, enough." Hunter employs that gentle, stern tone only he can—but there's something off in its cadence. I've never heard this grit in his voice before. This...hate. "Snowy," he says gently, "you will press charges."

"Charges?" Ronan fumes. "I'll kill that son of a bitch—"

"I can't breathe." My fingers clutch at my chest as if physical touch can force air into it. Suddenly, Ronan is by my side, rubbing my shoulders.

"It's okay, Snowy," he croaks. "We'll make this better. I'll fix this."

"We need to put out a statement," Hunter suggests. "Something concise—"

"Please." I pull away from them, heading for my room. "I just…I just need to think."

I might as well have said nothing, because they continue to talk without me. Shout. Argue.

Closing my door only muffles the sounds, not that I can shut out the world so easily. The paper taunts me from my bed. It's as if the honking horns and faint clamor of traffic below carry the vicious rumors directly to my ears.

I look forward to the tabloids, Snow.

Someone must have recorded us. Someone who leaked select phrases to the papers. But why? Dazed and dizzy, I can't come up with a single name. The only thing I'm sure of is guilt. It hammers through my veins in time with my heartbeat. Liar. Liar. Liar.

You've ruined his life twice, Snowy.

Hunter claimed that his spot on the board is already in jeopardy. I should be happy to hear that. Maybe if I were a real Hollings, I would be. Scandal festers like a poison in a city like Mayfield. Losing the company would only be the first cog in the vicious wheel of public contempt. Only God knows what could happen next.

Could he lose his money?

His home?

More?

I'm pacing again, wringing my fingers together, desperate to do something. Eventually, I find myself near my door, feeling along the wood. The shouting sounds fainter now; Ronan and Hunter must be in another room.

Heart pounding, I approach my closet and throw on the first items of clothing I can reach. Jeans. A blouse. Once dressed, I open my door and creep beyond it.

I don't see Ronan or Hunter within view, and I reach the door to the suite without drawing notice. Leaving now is the worst possible thing I could do. I know it, but my body doesn't seem to care. Rebelliously, my fingers clench the handle, turning it before my brain can fully process the consequences. Then I step out into the hall, and the moment I've cleared the threshold, I race into an elevator.

My thoughts are a jumble as I exit the lobby minutes later. Dazed, I find myself flagging down the first taxi I can, but once inside, I'm forced to admit that I don't even know where to go.

Or do I?

Without thinking, I blurt out a single address. Regret sinks in the moment the cab approaches a reclusive manor on the outskirts of Mayfield. Or it once *was* reclusive.

Now, a herd of news vans is swarming outside the gates.

"Holy shit!"

I flinch as the driver voices the concerns I don't dare.

"Are you sure about this, lady?"

Am I? An answer won't leave my throat. In the end, I just nod.

"All right." With a wary glance at me, the driver presses on.

The car barely travels a few feet before unknown faces press against the windows of the taxi. Cameras flash as pounding fists and shouting voices demand answers.

"Do you know Blake Lorenz?"

"I think it's her!"

"Ms. Hollings! Ms. Hollings!"

Thankfully, the wrought-iron gates barring the road part as if on cue, and the driver fearlessly peels through them. Far too soon, the sprawling manor house looms on the horizon. The chaos hasn't reached here, at least. Imposing and dark, the house looks more untouched than it did two months ago.

After paying the fare with what little cash I have on me, I cautiously approach the front door and lift the lion-shaped door knocker. No one responds to the first knock though. Uneasy for reasons I can't explain, I switch to knocking with my fists.

Still no answer.

So I try again, pounding. Banging.

Words meld into my attempts before I can bite them back. "Blake? Blake, please—"

A lock disengages, and the door opens so quickly that my fist meets air. Momentum draws me forward, right into the body of a figure who palms my waist, effortlessly righting my balance.

"I'm surprised you're here."

I look up, inhaling sharply. He's paler than I've seen him yet, outlasting the dark. Mussed hair and reddened eyes betray the depth of his exhaustion. His expression, however, reveals nothing. No anger. No shock, either.

"Come to see for yourself?" He steps back and pauses as if giving me the chance to run.

I should. God knows why I inch forward instead, allowing him to close the door behind me, which drenches us in shadow.

He hasn't lightened his decor any. The house remains dark, but before where his servant, Charles, added at least the illusion of a lived-in dwelling, I now sense only silence. He's alone.

Why that thought makes my heart pound harder? I don't know.

"What are you doing here, Snow?"

"I didn't..." My voice thickens and I swallow hard to strengthen it. "The recordings. I didn't release them. I swear—"

"There's no need to waste your breath," he says.

My heart sinks. This was a mistake. Stung, I start for the door, but his hand brushes my arm, drawing me back.

"Wait. I… I believe you."

"Y-you do?" I blink, unable to recognize the stranger watching me, devoid of hate and rage. God, he looks so damn tired.

Even his lips seem to have barely enough energy to twitch into a frown. "There are other ways you could hurt me, Snow."

How so? By revealing his true identity?

Hooded eyes reveal no answers. Instead, he turns on his heel and wanders deeper into the house. "But maybe now we can talk, at least."

Talk? I follow him despite my better judgment, keeping enough of a distance that he's beyond my reach. I examine him visually instead.

His clothing is wrinkled, a suit that looks more than a day old. His hair has been ruthlessly ravaged by his raking fingers. The disheveled air is such a far cry from the cold, polished man I know him as, and I'm drawn closer by a dangerous step. A single brush of my hand along his forearm reveals crackling tension trapped beneath his skin. I try to pull away, but he turns, grabbing my wrist. One tug lures me closer as his free hand captures my chin, forcing me to meet his gaze. With surprising tenderness, he tilts my face toward his.

"I'm ruined, Snow," he murmurs as if marveling at the term. "I bet you and your brothers are ecstatic. You always did love a bit of poetic irony. I've burned your name to elevate mine, and now look at us both—"

"Don't say that." My heart aches, more so because of cruel memory. *Poetic irony.* It's something Brandt would say. I shake my head to clear it, desperate to stay on topic. "I'm not here to gloat. I just... What can I do?"

Helping him should be the least of my worries. In fact, given everything he's done, I have more than enough reason to hate him. If only my heart knew that too. I look at him and try to only see Blake Lorenz. I *try.*

But his eyes—the brief glimpse of them I catch from behind a wayward lock of his hair—draw a different answer to my lips.

"A press conference," I find myself proposing. "I could say something. Say that my words were misconstrued—"

"No." He shakes his head. "That wouldn't work."

"Then what?" I grit my teeth, desperate to do *something.* Anything.

"There is something..." He turns away as if repulsed by the idea before he's even voiced it. "We'd need to be seen." When I say nothing, his eyes cut to mine, brimming with intensity. "We'd have to convince them that I never hurt you. Or," he adds as if sensing the memories playing on the fringes of my thoughts, "we'd convince them that you've forgiven me."

Forgiven. I stare blankly ahead as my mind spins with the term. After all he's done to me, can I afford such a luxury?

"I'd have to be seen with you," he reiterates. "Could you do it?"

A better question is: Can *he* after all I've done to him? The man who can't seem to look at me without baring his teeth in hatred. Could he set that aside, if only to clear his name?

Lost in thought, I gaze out a nearby window. A drab, gray sky promises a storm. I sense it hovering on the horizon, waiting to break. Every fiber of my being tells me to leave now. Avoid the tempest. Run. But, when I glance over and meet his gaze, something in me shifts. He looks so human in this moment, almost like a stranger. Someone older than Brandt yet softer than Blake. Someone vulnerable.

I nod. "Y-yes. I think I can try."

His jaw tightens, highlighting the gauntness of his features. "Good. I know it won't be easy."

"It won't be," I agree. Swallowing hard, I square my chin. "Which is why I want something in return."

He stiffens. "What?"

"You allow my brothers onto the board when your position is secure." I pause, but he doesn't shout or deny me outright. Odd. Inhaling deeply, I soldier on. "You can hate me all you want, but don't punish them. Please."

"Damn it... I don't hate you." He tears a hand through his hair as if grappling with that admission the same way I am.

My shoulders slump beneath a sudden sense of weightlessness, and I'm forced to cling to the wall for balance.

"Maybe I never did. Maybe..." He sighs, his teeth gritted, and shakes his head. "Doesn't matter. Fine. But, in exchange, I want something from you as well."

"What?" A part of me suspects the answer even before he directs a searching glance in my direction.

"A single night won't be enough. Not to convince everyone. You once promised me an entire year..."

"No." Horror robs my voice of any strength. The protest just resonates as a formless whisper. I cringe beneath the assault of memories: the pain, the humiliation, the shame. The sex. The nights that still leave me jolting awake, gasping at their intensity. I barely lasted a month of our previous arrangement.

"It wouldn't be like before," he says, his tone hard. "I won't... We'd just have to convince them in public. You'd still have your freedom, Snow."

Freedom. My breath catches at how valuable he makes that word sound. As if it's the world's most coveted possession. He's offering it to me willingly. I'd be a fool to turn him down. I sense all of those sentiments in everything he doesn't say.

But then there is the small matter of what he has said. I hate you, Snow. I'll break you, Snow. I own you, Snow. Did you really think I'd let you keep it?

"I want it in writing."

He inhales sharply, betraying his irritation at the ultimatum. So used to holding the cards, he can't stand to let one slip out of play. "I'll write you a check," he says, palming the pocket of his slacks as if he intends to do just that. "How is that for binding?"

"For how much?" I blurt before I can help myself. A heartbeat later, I add, "Nothing you say is binding."

Lightning-fast anger flickers across his face, disappearing almost as quickly. "Well, considering that *you* are the one in control of the situation…"

He waits while I process just what he means.

I can make my own demands.

"I want it in writing," I reiterate. "You guarantee my brothers a spot on the board. And—"

"What else?" he prompts. "Make your demands."

"I want full control over what I wear," I say in a rush. "How I dress. How I act. You demand nothing."

No illicit commands. No demeaning acts. No taunts or vicious games revolving around my weight.

He processes my words coldly, his frown unnerving. "And if I refuse?"

Then so do I. The words spring to the tip of my tongue, but I fail to voice them. On the surface, I could leave him to ruin. But my brothers and I would be no better off. Sure,

Blake could be removed from the board, but there is no guarantee that the remaining members would choose to reinstate a Hollings in his place. I'd still be a pauper with no money to my name, and he'd have no reason to bargain. With one expert twist, he's proven to be a calculating businessman. I have no choice but to play this game at least partially by his rules.

A satisfied gleam settles in his gaze as if he's aware of every thought twisting through my head. "I suggest you meet me halfway," he says. "A better arrangement for both parties."

"And what do you want?" I lick my lips in anticipation of the answer.

"Don't look so worried." It's an admonishment, not a taunt. "I won't have you do anything you don't want to. I simply need…assurance."

"Oh?"

"Of your safety." He's worried. For me? "Do you really think some lax hotel suite can protect you from a man like Lyle Harlow?"

I stiffen at the reference. All this time, I've fought to put my minor indiscretion out of my mind. As long as I didn't think about it, the danger didn't seem to matter. How fucking naïve.

But I won't have Blake Lorenz be the one to remind me of that foolishness.

"Then what do you suggest?" I counter. "That I stay with you?"

What I intend to be a cruel joke lands to a startling silence. Only a second passes before I realize that, yes, that's exactly what he intends. At least he has the decency not to say as much out loud. Instead, he raises an eyebrow and his mouth twitches as if fighting to keep from twisting into a frown.

"Would it really be so unbearable?" he wonders. "You'd be safer with me."

"Safe?" I rasp the word, but even I have enough tact not to mention the obvious.

How safe was I the night he set my home on fire with us inside it? How safe was I every night he tormented me with cruel insinuations or threats of physical violence? How safe am I here, with him now?

I hunt his eyes for an answer but find nothing but shadow. He's more alarming like this than he is raging with fury. At least then I know what to expect.

"The choice is up to you," he says on the cusp of a sigh. He even has the nerve to shrug—but I know him, this strange, vengeful creature he's become.

My heart lurches at the thought of just what he could have in store. There are so many corridors here for him to chase me around. So many rooms to hunt me in. So many chances to finish what he started.

"We wouldn't stay here." He scowls at the hallway's enclosed interior. "I own a penthouse downtown. It's centrally located. You can continue your affairs from there."

My affairs? I suspect he's referring to Haven. Good. I force myself to add, "I'd also like you to make a regular donation—"

"Done," he says, cutting me off. "But I want you to suggest to Riley Haverty that I become a primary benefactor."

I choke on any smugness I may have felt for leveraging Haven against him. "W-why?"

He shrugs again, turning to stare out the window. "You're not the only one with crusades. Riley Haverty is a shrewd businesswoman, but she's very wary of her contacts—for good reason."

"And, now, given the current news cycle, she wouldn't consult with you in a million years," I surmise.

"Something like that."

"Fine." It feels so strange to speak in such businesslike terms. I never was a part of the corporate world like my brothers. I never wanted to be. How ironic that I've been forced overnight to learn the ways of the boardroom, but they're applied in secret with a man who makes me tremble. I'd laugh if the prospect weren't so utterly pathetic. "So, what now?"

"Now..."

I stiffen as his footsteps grace the wood in tandem, drifting in my direction. Warmth alludes to the hand he brushes against my shoulder. Gently, as if he's aware I'll cringe from his reach. A part of me doesn't mean to. But my reactions to him are based on pure instinct. Muscle memory. I cringe. I shiver. I endure.

Surprisingly, he lets me scuttle away to a distant end of the hall. After a heartbeat of silence, he advances just a single step—to reinforce his presence, I suspect. He may pretend that I hold the cards, but there's no illusion here; he still runs the game.

"Now, we make our first move," he says, suddenly switching to a tone that reminds me of Papa. Calculating. "The world will be watching, demanding answers. I say we circumvent them. We take our 'relationship' public for a quiet night on the town, as if the rumors mean nothing."

I frown at the imagery. Only he would propose such a thing —someone with a wealth of confidence who has never been the butt of a cruel joke. Though maybe he has. I keep forgetting the truth behind his current persona. The differences between him and the boy he used to be are so vast that it's easy to forget they were the same person once. My beautiful Brandt Lloyd whose world I plunged into hell.

"Okay," I say thickly. "Just how do we do that?" I look over my shoulder and find him staring pensively into the air, stroking his chin with the pad of his thumb.

"I have an idea in mind. Leave the arrangements to me."

"I thought *we*"—I stress the word—"were in this together."

"We are." He sounds surprised by my doubt. "But just... just let me take the lead just this once. I promise to consult you from then on."

I find myself gritting my teeth, anxious at the thought. In the end, I don't have much of a choice. "What am I supposed to do?"

He smiles, but there's no joy in it. His eyes remain distant, focused on something far beyond me. "In the meantime, you play the part," he says. "It's best if you get dressed here, however, given the current circumstances."

A part of me agrees, unwilling to cross the horde of paparazzi alone. "But," I start, "I don't have any clothing here."

Somehow, I know even before I see the slight tilt of his chin that he's one step ahead, like always.

"I have a few things that may be in your size," he says softly. "They're upstairs. First door on the left."

Things of his sister's? Another woman's? I don't have the nerve to ask. Instead, I jump at the chance to escape him, even if it's just by a few yards.

The upper level of his home is no less intimidating than the entrance. Shadows drape the winding hallway, and most of the doors are closed, including the one he directed me to. I open it warily as my stomach knots at the thought of what may lurk behind it.

Once I finally peer inside the room, a gasp escapes my throat. Someone unloaded racks and racks of designer clothing into what must have been a guest room.

All are mine. The shoes stacked neatly on the floor are mine. In fact, the longer I stare, the more I recognize every item from my old room at Hollings Manor.

My dressers.

My vanity.

My old mirror.

So this is where he kept them.

I don't know if I'd prefer he'd thrown it all away. This wardrobe belongs to a stranger, one who prioritized beauty over compassion or common sense. She lived her life looking only to sparkle, heedless of the damage she left in her wake.

I don't know who I've become in the few short months since having this persona stripped away.

Drawing in a ragged breath, I step into the guest room and close the door. After a moment's pause, I lock it. Then I wander from each rack of clothing, surveying my options. So many things to choose from, yet none of them catch my eye. In the end, I select a modest navy ensemble with a high neckline and long sleeves. I suspect, even before I strip my outfit and pull it on, that it isn't what Blake Lorenz had in mind when he ordered me to play my role.

He wanted Snowy Hollings, the charming socialite. But it's getting harder and harder to be her.

Sure enough, when I finally creep from the room and approach the staircase, I find him watching me from the bottom step. His expression reveals nothing. Neither do his eyes as they perform a slow perusal of the body-hugging yet simple dress. Finally, he nods as if to convey: *As you wish.*

"I made us a reservation," he says.

Only now do I realize that he's changed as well, into a simple black suit with a crimson tie. We don't match in the slightest, a fact that lingers at the back of my mind. He's dressed to kill, while I'm...

I'm dressed like prey who's already been savaged.

"Wait." I turn on my heel, leaving him in the foyer.

Upon returning to the blue room, I head straight to a rack I initially overlooked. Hanging near the very back is a gown I once purchased with one sole purpose in mind: capture my ex-fiancé, Daniel Ellingston. We needed the money, and like the perfect tool, Hunter put me to the task. I did my duty well enough that within one meeting I'd already secured a date and a slew of roses hand-delivered to my home the following day. Now, it's merely a befitting piece of armor to wear into this new war. Blake Lorenz doesn't own me—not anymore.

This time, I dress slowly, ensuring that every curve is accented perfectly by silk and lace. I find an adjacent bathroom and arrange my hair around my shoulders. Left with no makeup, I pinch color into my cheeks and bite my lips until they redden. With one last glance at myself, I return to the front of the house.

Observing the man watching my descent, I know I've done my duty well. He clutches the banister so tightly that his knuckles whiten. *Damn.* I'm not sure if he truly grates the word between his teeth or if I imagine it. Either way, his blue-eyed gaze hunts me with every inch of space I cover between us. When I finally reach his side, I shiver before he even attempts to bring his hand against my lower back.

"Not here," I croak, loathing the fear I can't contain. Not here, alone, where his nearness grates on what little composure I have left.

Without a word, he approaches the front door and opens it, revealing a car already idling in the driveway. A single nod ushers me after him and into our first battle.

SIX

I CAN TASTE the tension on my tongue as the car starts down the driveway, approaching the reporters gathered at the front gate. Once more, eager faces press against the windows, fighting for a glimpse beyond the tinted glass.

"You get used to being a public spectacle," Blake explains, eyeing my trembling hands. "Show them fear and they become relentless."

A hard swallow contorts my throat. "I remember."

Admittedly, my father's legal team kept the worst of the reporters at bay back then, but the boy I accused of the unthinkable wasn't so lucky. No wonder he seems so unaffected by the chaos around him now.

"We'll have dinner," he says as if sensing the direction my thoughts have taken. Obsessive control is perhaps the one trait of Brandt's he still possesses, only magnified times a million. I sense the chains of his plan wrapping around me, tethering me to an unknown outcome. "Then I'll have your things brought to the penthouse."

I don't miss how he avoids the defining nature of said penthouse: *his* penthouse.

"That's not necessary." A night tops. That's how much I'll give him. A night spent awake, hoping my brothers don't beat their way inside with their bare fists—or with the aid of a SWAT team. Speaking of Ronan and Hunter... "My brothers want your blood, you do realize." And for a good reason. "How am I supposed to convince them that we are not only reconciled, but cordial? They think—"

"Leave it to me," he says. I'm alarmed by just how confident he sounds, though at a glance, his expression reveals nothing. "And I will go ahead with having your things moved. Unless you've decided to purchase new clothing."

"Shopping hasn't been my focus as of late," I admit. "And I wouldn't want to impose—"

"Don't fight me on this." There's no anger in his tone, a fact that only unnerves me. He sounds so damn serious. As if, somewhere beneath that frosty exterior, he may give a damn about me.

Or maybe it's his image. If I get murdered by Lyle Harlow, he'll be the one suspicion falls upon first.

"You really think I should stay with you?" I find myself asking.

A harsh exhale escapes his clenched teeth. I look over and find his hands tightening into fists only to suddenly unfurl and settle over his lap.

"I'll let you decide that for yourself after tonight."

The offer feels less like a show of faith and more like an ominous dare. Still, I say nothing during the rest of the trek into the heart of Mayfield.

By "handle things," it quickly becomes apparent that Blake meant "ensure that the world knows exactly where to find us."

Our destination is visible from blocks away due to the paparazzi stationed at the building's entrance. I vaguely recognize the restaurant as one of the most premier establishments in town. Blake Lorenz must still carry enough sway, even while disgraced, to command a table here. Especially now.

"This shouldn't take long," Blake assures me as the driver cuts through the calamity to bring us as close to the restaurant's entrance as possible.

How he knows as much, I don't dare ask. Instead, I fidget, tugging at my gown, suddenly aware of its low neckline. What an affront to anyone who'd dare pity me as a victim I make: stepping out with my supposed abuser, wearing the dress of a foolish socialite as if oblivious to scandal. Perhaps that's why Blake seems so satisfied by the costume change.

As the driver parks and circles around to his end, he reaches for me, but I flinch out of his range.

"I'm fine."

His low sigh cuts the air, resonating restraint. "Appearances, Snow," he says simply.

Left with no choice, I force my hand against his, and he grips it tight. Then, together, we exit the car to a myriad of shouted questions and statements.

"Ms. Hollings! Is it true that you…"

"Is it true that he…"

"Mr. Lorenz, are you a predator?"

To his credit, the man weathers it all with barely a frown to show for it, but he tightens his grip, ruthlessly steering me forward as strangers crowd in.

"No one will harm you," he swears.

Almost as if on cue, imposing men in suits swarm from nowhere to flank us on four sides, keeping the crowd at bay. He wasn't lying about being prepared.

I can't escape the suspicion that he's planned everything, down to ensuring that a restaurant employee would usher us inside while firmly keeping all others out.

"Reservation only," he mutters.

Together, we enter a partially deserted dining room filled with just a few couples who barely look up from their elegant meals. Odd. Even the poshest of socialites I know can't resist the obvious allure of a scandal. Unless, of course, they weren't socialites at all.

Confused, I glance at Blake from the corner of my eye as he leads me to a table in the room's very center. Draped in an ivory tablecloth, it serves as the perfect stage for a couple's intimate dinner.

"Why do I get the feeling that nothing in this room is authentic?" I ask in a fitting stage-whisper.

He shrugs before gesturing to the waiter approaching us with a bottle of wine. "That's because it isn't. The other diners are actors and the waiter is in my employ."

"Are you serious?"

He raises an eyebrow, but I can't tell if he's amused or joking. "Have a seat."

Resigned, I claim the chair he's pulled out for me and watch him circle the table. Seated, he towers over the elegant table setting—a baron lording over this room and all inside it.

"I thought we were supposed to be convincing?"

A slight quirk tilts his lips. Just as quickly, he's blank again, eyeing me as the waiter fills two crystal glasses with wine. "That will come later. Trust me."

I swallow hard. "Fine. And in the meantime?"

He nods to our empty place settings. "Try to relax."

It's like he's in my head, sensing the nerves I can't suppress.

I cast a wary glance around the room, taking in its muted but chic color scheme of black and silver. Last I heard, most had to wait on the guest list for months to earn a table here.

Barely a few months in Mayfield and Blake Lorenz has already scored the chef's table.

"You came back." I clear my throat, unsure of how else to phrase it. Came back. As if he ever had a choice in leaving. "How... Your sentence. They told me that you..."

He reaches across the table for the wrapped silverware in front of me and effortlessly unfurls the white napkin from the utensils. Without prompting, he sets my fork and knife on either side of my plate. Then he flicks the napkin into the air but stops short of placing it on my lap for me. Instead, he sets it aside and withdraws to his end of the table.

"It's complicated," he says carefully. I don't miss how he reaches up to adjust his tie, a rare display of unease. "I'd rather not discuss it here."

"Oh." Am I disappointed? Or was I so foolish to suspect he might feel obligated to tell me something about his past? A gap of ten years separates who we are now from the children we used to be. I'd give anything for at least a glimpse at what the darkness in his gaze shrouds—if only to know how to better protect myself against it. "How can you even sit there?" I wonder, a blunter way of phrasing: *I thought you hated me. Despised me, even.*

His mouth twists into a wry frown. "I'll let you know the answer when I figure it out myself."

Fair enough. At least it's not a lie: *I forgive you.* "So..." I clear my throat, hunting for a change in conversation. "You have a sister?"

His fleeting frown warns me of yet another topic determined to be off-limits. "I've had them cook your favorites," he says rather than mention Masha.

I turn and find a waiter carrying two meals on a tray. The first is a modest steak adorned with grilled vegetables. On the other is a small pile of pasta primavera paired with a toasted piece of French bread. A small slice of strawberry shortcake accompanies it.

"You remembered," I say thickly. "Thank you. But I'm not hungry."

Something unreadable darkens his expression. When I don't touch my food, he doesn't reach for his, either. We're at an impasse, watching each other from above steaming plates.

"You're afraid to eat in front of me," he says suddenly.

My cheeks flush, and I shake my head. It's like I still hear him hissing into my ear: *He hated you, not because you were disgusting*.

"For what it's worth…I apologize now for—"

"We can discuss it later," I blurt. Only belatedly do I realize that I've just thrown his own words right back in his face.

His eyebrows rise slightly as a low chuckle rumbles from his chest. "Little Snow, always so manipulative." Suddenly, he pushes back from the table and begins to unfurl his silverware. "Ask me what you wish as you enjoy your meal. Our 'dinner' won't seem convincing if you don't eat."

Ah. I don't dare question the tit for tat. My stomach churns at the thought of eating now, of all times. But I'll do anything for answers. Slowly, I break off a piece of bread and bring it to my lips. "Blake Lorenz," I say before taking a bite. After swallowing, I add, "Who was he?"

"My real father," he says. His fingers manipulate his bundle of silverware. Within seconds, he has the utensils free and the napkin folded neatly on his lap. "He was a prominent businessman in Germany. My mother must have had the affair before she married Harrison Lloyd. After my conviction, she contacted him. He used his influence to have 'Blake Lorenz' enrolled in the facility as my cellmate. Not long after, 'Brandt Lloyd' committed suicide and Blake was released on a technicality. His only stipulation was that I leave my life in America behind."

"So you moved to Germany." It's not hard to picture him then, maneuvering the foreign landscape. He was always adept at mastering most social situations.

"I kept abreast of what happened in Mayfield," he says. "I knew when my mother died, and Harrison Lloyd. And Elizabeth…"

My mother. A woman I'm starting to realize he knew better than I ever did. "Why didn't you ever tell me about her?"

He cuts his gaze down to my plate. Reluctantly, I scrape a bit of noodle onto my fork and take a bite.

"Would you have believed me?" he counters as I swallow. "I hated Harrison Lloyd. Your world *revolved* around Forrest

Hollings."

And, in a way, it still does. Papa rules our entire lives from the grave, dictating our one worth—as a Hollings always. I wonder now for the first time if he ever suspected the truth. Perhaps knowing I wasn't his child made it easier for him to hurt me…

"Snow?"

"Hmm?" I blink back tears, looking up. He's watching me, and I'm not brave enough to wonder for how long. "My mother. You always knew about her affair?" I ask while stabbing at another piece of food.

"For years," he admits. "And I didn't tell you about her for obvious reasons."

If my life revolved around Forrest, then it was balanced upon Elizabeth. Thinking of her in anything less than a flattering light stings. All of those memories feel tainted by the awful truth. She lied to me. Even worse, through me; she ruined Brandt irreparably.

"I would have never given her my letters," I admit around a lump in my throat. "If I had known, I would have—"

"I know." He grabs his knife and carves a slice from his steak. It's rare inside, leaving a pinkish smear of fluid across the plate. "It won't be easy, but… I'm trying to put that in the past."

But can we? I can't stop my fingers from tracing the right side of my face, the scar still healing there. His eyes catch the motion, and the knife rattles to the table. Suddenly, his hand cups mine.

"I never wanted to hurt you."

The depth of the admission unnerves me, almost as much as my reaction to it does. I stop breathing. Thinking. His heat is a trigger to a million sensations, each one more destructive than the last.

"Yes, you did," I find myself replying. Very slowly, I pull away from his touch, guarding my wound with the flat of my palm.

A sharp noise cuts the air like that of teeth clicking together. Then his throat contracts around a hard swallow. "I did," he says.

And we ignore our plates in unison.

Sweat drips down my back, seeping into the priceless gown. Thinking we could normally coexist in any capacity was a mistake. Too many secrets taint the air. Too many old emotions burn when disturbed. My eyes sting, but blinking hastens the tears forming. Far too quickly, they seep from their hiding places and slide down my cheeks.

"Shit, *enough*." Before I can react, he's closer, swiping at my tears, frowning as he does so. "So much for forgiveness, huh?" he murmurs, scowling at his glistening fingers.

I can't find the words to argue, and he says nothing else. Neither does he remove his hand, and I don't have the strength to pull away. In his eyes, I see a vortex of emotions impossible to decipher. A part of me wants to try anyway, anything to understand him. Guilt? Remnants of anger? Pain?

Sighing, he tilts my chin against his thumb, observing me from the newer angle. "I'll admit it now," he says, his voice a rasp. "I didn't seek you out before solely to warn you about Harlow. There's something else. I want something from you."

My stomach falls. Smashes into pieces on the floor. I inhale raggedly, wary of what he could say. A real apology? Something far more sinister?

Indigo irises search mine as his lips finally part. "I want us to start over, Snow—"

Breaking glass and a monstrous thud add an eerily beautiful melody to his plea. Suddenly, he draws back, rising to his feet—just in time for a bulky blur to ram into him, knocking him off-balance. I blink in shock as the "blur" rapidly takes on more human characteristics: blond hair, blazing blue eyes, flying fists, striking any part of Blake they can reach.

Oh, God.

"Ronan!" I shout, but he doesn't seem to hear me.

He keeps fighting, pummeling Blake, who does his best to block every blow. Growling, Ronan catches him in the mouth with his knuckles. Blood flies, splattering the fronts of expensive suits.

"Ronan, stop!" I stagger to my feet and paw at his shoulder. Grunting, he shrugs me off. Another of his blows lands with a thud, this time in Blake's stomach. "Stop!"

Maybe it's my scream that does it, but Ronan suddenly stumbles back. At the same time, he grabs my arm, wrenching me around to face him. "What in the hell are you doing here with *him*?"

I'm struck dumb as my brother glares from me to Blake.

"I see you near her again, I'll fucking kill you—"

"Stop it!" I manage to break his grip, and I scramble out of his reach before he can grab me again. "Ronan, calm down."

I barely recognize him. Blood speckles his chin, but it's not his. No, the only bleeding figure is the one currently watching the exchange while swiping at his mouth with the back of his hand. His bottom lip is split, and redness around his left eye tells me it won't stay any color but purple for much longer.

"Get over here, Snowy," my brother demands.

My chest constricts around fragile lungs, which makes it impossible to suck in air. I only have enough breath to croak, "Ronan, it isn't what it looks like. What the papers printed were lies. He never hurt me—"

"Snowy." He's begging, something I rarely see him do—and never like this. Veins bulge against the skin of his neck as his hands clench into fists. His gaze cuts to Blake again, and I scramble to put myself between them.

"I promise I'll explain!" I say, placing my hand on Ronan's chest. "Just trust me. Please. Trust me."

"Then come home." He reaches for me, but I once again evade his reach.

Why? I don't know. If there was ever a reason to ignore Blake's proposal, it's this: I can't bear to see Ronan so furious.

"I will," I tell him, my voice breaking. "But just give me time to explain. I promise I will."

"We need to go."

I stiffen. Blake doesn't even have to speak in my ear for his voice to resonate through me, invading every nerve. From the corner of my eye, I see him paces back, still swiping at his bleeding mouth. The reminder is clear: I have a bargain to uphold.

"Like hell!" Ronan bares his teeth and postures as if preparing to lunge. "You aren't taking her anywhere, you sick piece of shit—"

"*Snow.*"

"W-wait." I glance at my brother, willing him to listen to me. "I'll be okay. I promise." Turning from Ronan, I extend my hand to the man behind me. "Let's go."

He's by my side in an instant. Before I realize it, we're hurrying from the restaurant doors, with Ronan close behind. When I hear him shout, I look back and find that

Blake's bodyguards have appeared from nowhere to keep him at bay.

"He'll be fine," Blake murmurs into my ear. Without giving me the time to protest, he ushers me into the back seat of the car and the driver takes off.

Neon streetlights cast the back seat in a reddish glow. Only as my vision blurs do I finally register the moisture slicking my cheeks.

"Do it now," I say, my voice breaking. "Uphold your end of the bargain and put them back on the board. Do it now!"

He already has a cell phone against his ear. After a few minutes of murmured conversation, he hangs up and tosses the phone onto the seat between us. "It's done."

My shoulders slump. A sliver of power perhaps wouldn't be enough to console any other brother, but I know mine. Intrigue alone will buy me more time to explain. What, exactly? I'm not sure.

Perhaps how I lost my senses enough to trust Blake Lorenz for a second time.

"Where are we going?" I ask, not recognizing this part of town where skyscrapers tower above.

He casts me a glance that could be described as equal parts amused and irritated. "Home," he says. "My penthouse. I took the liberty of having your things delivered."

Despite my having explicitly told him not to. For now, I don't challenge him. Instead, I try to decipher every twist and turn and remember every street name, just in case I have to make my way back to the hotel on foot. Normally, I'd laugh at such a dramatic thought. However, going off the blood still dripping from the mouth of the man beside me, I think the theatrics are warranted.

"You're hurt."

He frowns and brings a hand to his bottom lip. The fingers come away red, glistening in the glow of a passing streetlamp.

"Oh God, here." I run a hand down the side of my gown but find nothing useful.

Motion catches the corner of my eye, and I find him fishing a handkerchief from his pocket. He holds it awkwardly between his chin and his chest as if unsure whether to clean himself or…

"Let me." I snatch the cloth and shift closer, pressing it against the worst of the bleeding.

He flinches, his eyes tracking every movement of my fingers.

"You'll have a scar," I tell him, impressed by the veracity of the wound. Ronan has a vengeful streak, but I've never seen him attack someone before. Not even the bullies who taunted me all those years ago. No, that honor always went to another boy who once punched a bully who'd lifted my skirt in grade school to see how fat I was underneath.

Something in my face must change, because my fingers are gently batted away.

"I've got it," Blake says, adjusting the cloth to staunch even more of the bleeding. Protocol would dictate that I apologize to him on Ronan's behalf.

But I don't.

In silence, we endure the rest of the ride until the car enters a secluded parking garage and comes to a stop near an elevator.

"The suite has a private entrance," Blake explains as he exits the car, this time without reaching for my hand.

I follow him warily, tense for reasons I can't explain. It's quiet here, which is an eerie contrast to the chaos of his home in the hills and the restaurant. He must keep this residence unlisted, a prospect that unnerves me more than it should. Just how many secrets is he hiding?

Speaking of which.

"Is Masha here?" I wonder, feigning innocence. "I'd hate to intrude."

Blake enters the elevator, leaving me to follow. "No," he says without looking back. "I have her staying someplace far beyond the city."

Fair enough. I picture what little I can remember of the blond waif who claimed to be his sister. She's beautiful, that much I'm sure of. And she's young.

"You're doubting if I've told you the whole truth."

I jump and look up. His narrowed gaze meets mine unflinchingly.

"She is my sister," he reiterates without voicing my suspicion out loud. "My half-sister, but my sister nonetheless."

"How old is she?" I ask, watching him strike the button for the top floor.

"She…" He hesitates as the elevator car lurches beneath us. I'm seconds from admitting defeat when he sighs. "She's twenty."

"Oh." I swallow hard. So she *is* young. "And she grew up in Germany?"

"Exclusively," he says, eyeing the doors, his jaw rigid. "I met her there when she was still a child. Twelve, I think."

Which makes for a two-year gap between his supposed death as Brandt Lloyd and his rebirth as Blake Lorenz. In the end, I decide against commenting on that point. Instead, I tilt my chin, observing him as closely as I dare.

He's different when he speaks of Masha versus anyone else, even me. There's a softness about him. A wariness, as if he isn't sure just what his face might reveal.

"Speaking of Masha…" He surges forward, leaving me to catch up. "She helped me design this place. I hope you don't mind the décor."

We follow a short hallway that leads directly into a spacious foyer.

And my mouth drops open.

Once upon a time, I used to babble to Brandt Lloyd about my hopes and dreams. I told him that I aspired to be an astronaut; in space, no one would give a damn about my weight. I told him about my dream home: a high-rise overlooking the heart of the city. *Like a castle for a princess*, I used to quip. One decorated in shades of emerald and gold, our favorite colors. But not gaudily, of course. Natural. Like a snapshot of a forest taken the split second before winter sets in. When everything is that silvery hue of stillness, and the air smells so clean that you can taste it. When greens never look greener, and the earth still holds that summery warmth.

"Masha" must have been there to overhear all of those silly daydreams, because the interior of this room feels ripped right from my fantasies. Gray marble floors add contrast to earth-colored walls. Black accents and silver fixtures cast a warm yet chilling atmosphere that demands any occupant to curl up with a book in one of the welcoming nooks. So many books line the shelves along a wall that opens onto a sitting room with floor-to-ceiling windows.

It's breathtaking. Literally. My hand flutters to my chest as if aiming to force air into it.

"I… It's beautiful." I don't mean to sound so damn awestruck. Neither can I stop myself from approaching the view and bracing my hands against the glass.

Something nearby catches my attention: a red leather chair angled toward the incredible swath of the city laid bare. Ice runs through my veins, displacing some of the wonder. "I'd want a throne, of course," I boasted once. "Red, placed perfectly to take in my servants…"

"I had a feeling you'd enjoy this." Blake seems unaware of my sudden realization as he comes to stand by my side. A rare smile shapes his mouth, visible in his reflection off the glass. Smug. "It's yours."

A watery laugh trickles from my throat. "Thank you, but I can't afford it."

"I'm serious." A sudden shift in his stance draws my attention a second time. He's standing rigidly, surveying the world glittering down below. "If you need a reason to trust me, then here: It's yours."

"Stop it!" I push back from the window and turn on my heel. The unfamiliar layout looms before me—so much for the hysterics. If I were to make a dramatic exit, I wouldn't even know which way to go. With my shoulders back and my breaths ragged, I settle on the next best thing and march toward the mouth of the foyer. "You don't have to ply me with expensive gifts or favors." Then a cruel thought strikes me, drawing a gasp from my lips. "I'm not the same selfish little girl I was—"

"And I don't want to hate that girl anymore." He seizes my arm from behind, yanking me against a body made of steel.

"D-don't!" Agony strikes a wounding blow on my heart. "Stop... Stop mocking me—"

"I'm *not*." His arm cinches my waist before I can run— and something keeps me from resisting. Perhaps it's how he sounds? Ragged breaths rake the air near my ear, betraying fracturing control I doubt he ever had a full grasp on. "I hurt you. I know I did," he rasps. "And I... We'll do this your way. Retribution. An eye for an eye. Tell me what you want from me. I'll give it to you. Anything—"

"All I want is the truth!" I sag against him as my voice echoes in the cavernous space, high-pitched and thready.

Rather than laughing, he nods, sliding his nose against the groove in my neck. "And you'll have it," he promises. "You will. I swear it. But I need something from you, Snow." He sounds like a drowning man begging for a lifeline. Rope. A bullet to the brain. Anything to ease his misery. Slowly, he loosens his grip on my waist but doesn't draw back. "I need five fucking minutes. That's all. Show me what I've lost. What I need to earn back."

His heated tone sends blood rushing to my cheeks. "You think... You really think you can ask me for sex—"

"Of course not." He scoffs, offended by the idea. "But I need... Show me what I've lost."

What he's lost? I pull away from him and find myself backing toward the window. Cool glass braces my spine, drawing my attention to just how thin this dress is. How fragile. Even so, it's thicker than my skin when it comes to him.

He wants to know what he's lost?

The moment I reach for a strap, he sucks in a breath. My thoughts run together, jumbled and incoherent. Lowering part of my dress is a foolish, stupid act. But it's all I have. The words won't come. Just tears. Just this pain contorting my features in ways I can't control. Slowly, I loosen the second strap and let the gown slide down my arms. I'm thin enough now that it falls without resistance and pools at my feet.

He told me once that he'd only want me while broken. While ugly. *His.* Apparently, he never lied in that respect. His jaw goes slack around a guttural groan, and he eyes me openly without shame, raking his gaze over my heaving chest and my trembling limbs.

I start to cover myself only to freeze when he shakes his head. Bitten-out words reverberate like thunder.

"You're so fucking beautiful…"

My cheeks heat at the raw tone. If only beauty weren't pain when it came to him. It's wrong, but I do it: I compare them. Brandt cherished and coddled sweet, lovely, beautiful things. Blake crushes them—something he seems inclined to do to me. I don't miss how his fingers twitch at his sides before he wrestles them against his hips.

"I won't touch you," he warns before surging forward, swallowing the distance between us.

My breath stills in my chest as I watch him advance, quivering on my heels. His eyes meet mine, the pupils dilated, while his body cages me against the glass. With our chests separated by just a fragile inch of space, he inhales me, bracing one hand against the glass near my head.

"Show me what I've damaged, Snow," he begs, his voice hollow. "Show me. I swear I won't touch you. I know I've hurt you. Tormented you…" Warm breath tickles my cheek, sending a ripple through my entire body, down to my toes. "Torment me."

My eyes shut, blocking his expression out as tension floods the air, soaking into every pore. Torment him? He desolated me. Not because of what he's said, or done, or inflicted. But because…

I'm weak.

I can't stop aching for what I'll never have, and I tell myself the brutal truth over and over. I'll never hear his voice reach that familiar, warm cadence. I'll never hear his laugh again, not like it was: soft and freeing. I'll never taste that innocent, sweet flavor that used to linger on his skin. I'll never taste Brandt Lloyd again. I'll never hear him groan…

Like the sound rumbling near my ear now. He'd sound softer, Brandt—never so hard. So empty. So hungry. Brandt Lloyd never lusted after me. He'd never watch me slide my fingers beneath the waistband of my panties just to test his response—explosive. Curses meet their doom, ground between clenched teeth.

I've never touched myself in front of anyone, not even him. Sweat slicks my skin, making it easier to follow the invisible trail down my stomach, toward the cleft between my legs. My cheeks catch fire at a sudden thought. How pathetic. This is as close as I'll ever get to my beautiful boy: a twisted reflection of who he used to be breathing his taint into my skin.

"Fuck," he rasps. "You're killing me."

Good. Some sick, vengeful part of me latches onto the genuine pain in his voice. I rock my hips against my fingers, biting my lip at the feeling. Hot. Wet. Then I stiffen in shock and draw my fingers away, the cold air licking at the moisture, raising goosebumps.

"Fuck." Something slams against the glass, rattling it, but he doesn't touch me. He keeps his promise, and I fight to uphold mine.

Torment him.

After what he's done to me, I want to take him up on his whispered exaggeration: I want to kill him. But I'm not sure how. Only that he groans again as I peel my panties down my legs. He's even closer now. His ragged breaths form a disjointed melody, counting the seconds down. With my bare ass against the window, I arch my hips, ensuring he can see every inch of the heated flesh. Torment him? With that goal in mind, I lazily flick my fingers along the heavy folds, relishing in the sensation he's denied himself. A low moan rips from my chest before I can swallow it down. My eyelids flutter, but I refuse to let them open. Not yet.

I rub, cupping myself against my palm, hating the fire that flares in response. God, his attention feels like groping, greedy fingers spreading me open for his pleasure. All I can do is retaliate, grinding my touch wherever I feel his gaze travel. Lower. Lower. Deeper...

"J-Jesus Christ." He barely sounds human—some growling creature salivating over a bone he can't have.

My body is a dirty traitor, however. It resists the finger I try to ease inside, clamping down, craving something larger. More forceful. Destructive.

"You're...killing...me...Snow." He sounds like he means it, which makes my heart despair. He sounds like he's enjoying every vicious bit of torture.

I bite my lip and forcefully ram the tip of my thumb inside. My gasp is swallowed by his growl. Vibrations ripple through the glass, but he never touches me. Not even when I give in to his plea. I rub. Twist. Curl. Fuck myself on the ridge of my own fingers. I let him watch. I let him moan, smothering the sound against what I assume is his palm.

Eventually, my body can't take any more. Fire ignites along my spine, forcing it to curl. Rudderless, I writhe against the glass. My knees buckle. Thoughts dissipate. When I regain my senses, I'm on my knees, shaking as footsteps resonate through the floor. Gasping, I look up and find him swaying on his feet, crossing the foyer.

"Get some rest," he croaks to me. "Your room is the first on the right, at the top of the stairs. I'll sleep in the study tonight."

A study that I assume is on the first floor, which gives me some ounce of distance from him. Alone, I haul myself to my feet and redress. Then I ascend the winding staircase, clinging to the banister for support. The top-level sports another breathtaking view of the cityscape, and leather chaises are positioned for viewing at the end of a wide hallway lined with several closed doors. I approach the one he directed me to and then grasp the handle.

I doubt Masha had a hand in designing *this* room, considering that its blue walls resemble the exact color scheme of my old room in Hollings Manor. The oak furniture is similar, and the door to the walk-in closet is open far enough to reveal my clothing hanging neatly on its racks.

I'm too overwhelmed to examine his motives for this gesture. Another taunt? I just close my eyes while locking the door behind me. Then I sink to the floor, my back pressed against the wall. I don't strip my gown or my heels. I don't seek out a comfortable position.

I test him, listening to his footsteps seep through the floor. And a strange thought sinks into my belly and won't leave: He picked this room for a reason, the one positioned directly above what I assume is his study. He knew I'd hear him through the walls. I could track his movements.

At the same time…

Even while alone, I'll never be able to ignore his presence.

SEVEN

BLAKE

I SPENT ten years pushing her away. Every thought. Every memory. I never looked at a picture of her. I never read an article.

For so damn long, I dwelled on the image of that silly little girl who threw my love away, and I purged that specter of everything that made her human.

Her smell.

Her touch.

The thought of her just triggered rage. Hatred. And I relished it.

She was the reason I fought so fucking hard to the top. The reason for every bastard crushed in my wake. My father's legacy was a fitting excuse, but it was her—loathing every inch of Snowy Hollings made each victory ten times sweeter.

One day, I'd swallow her entire world fucking whole.

But now...

The faintest hint of rose-scented perfume colors the air, even in here. My nostrils flare, hunting every last trace of the shit and I feel my brow furrow at the cloying aroma. It's her mother's smell. The old Snowy hated the scent of artificial flowers—she preferred to smell them fresh, drenched beneath a spring storm, or stolen from her family's gardens.

The Snowy Hollings I knew, was a writer, not a socialite. A girl who preferred to spill her emotions in poetry and stories scribbled in the margins of her father's books.

She was silly and so fucking trusting.

She was so damn *forgiving*.

I could ignore her on a bad day. Forget to walk her home. Casually insult her by accident with my careless fucking mouth.

She never once held any transgression against me.

To be fair, I always knew the right words to say, or gestures to make. I always knew *her*...

My pocket jolts, snapping me from my memory. Someone's calling and my jaw clenches. Only a handful of people in the entire fucking world would be so bold to disturb me this time of night.

One glance at the ID and I'm on my feet, my heart pounding so hard I can feel my pulse in every goddamn fingertip. "What is it?" I demand, answering.

The voice on the other end comes in snippets. "You promised. You promised me," a woman insists, sounding faint.

"Fuck." Panic rouses my pulse into a frantic, pounding rhythm. "Masha? Where are you?"

"You promised…" She must be outside. Rushing traffic snarls at her words, obscuring most of them. "Everything… my fault—"

"Where are you?" I lurch toward the door, fighting to keep my voice steady. "Tell me!"

"…never let me go," she insists, her voice broken by static. "I'm so sorry, Blake. He'll never…me go."

SNOWY

SHOUTING jars me awake and I scramble to my feet, struggling to get my bearings. Faint gray light adds little definition to my surroundings. For one cruel, sickening moment, I almost forget. I'm in Hollings Manor again, waking up late. My first instinct is to scramble into my bathroom to wash my face, but the moment I cross the threshold, reality returns. This layout is twice the size of my old bathroom, with a sunken tub and gold fixtures. In fact, every detail of this room seems designed to add a charm reminiscent of a deranged princess in a dark fairytale.

Shivering, I splash water on my face and rub my color back into my cheeks. I finger my hair and consider taking a risk by washing up even with Blake still so close.

I hear him pacing down below. Marching. Shouting?

Alarm draws me to the bedroom door. With my ear pressed against it, I can't make out what he's saying. Just the tone of how he's saying it: growled, frantic words bellowed in quick succession. He's arguing with someone. Then a terrible vision pops into my head: either Ronan or Hunter storming in, ready for a second round of what happened in the restaurant.

I'm already in the hallway before I can weigh the benefits of staying in hiding. In the pale light of dawn, I easily find my way to the staircase and into the foyer. There, I find him pacing just beyond the hall, a cell phone pressed to his ear, and his usually stoic expression radiating fury.

"What do you mean she's gone? Find her!" he snarls before rattling off a phrase that I don't think is English. "Did he call, that son of a bitch? No...the manor? What the hell was she doing out there? No, it doesn't matter. Don't let her out of your sight." A heartbeat later, the phone is flung from his grip and smashes against the wall inches from my head.

"Shit…" He deflates as if noticing me for the first time. A trembling hand does its best to rake a mess of black curls from his forehead only to make him look more disheveled. "I didn't see you. I-I have to go." He storms across the foyer to snatch a coat from a hook near the entrance. After shrugging it on, he cocks his head in my direction without turning around. "I'll be back later. Have your run of the place. Your breakfast is in the dining room."

Then he's gone, slamming the door in his wake.

It's like the very walls exhale the moment he's gone, and the beauty lurking in the muted color scheme makes itself known without the threat of him here to consume my attention. God, it's so beautiful. So dangerous. He turned my nostalgia into a weapon.

Or a cage.

Alone, I watch the world rouse from a sleepy trickle of traffic into a full-blown torrent of people and machines surging toward various goals. It's a view of the world I never got from my window at Hollings Manor. Though I always dreamt of moving to the heart of the city like the stereotypical socialite.

In the end, I never left home. I had to be smoked from the ruins of it, thrown into this louder, gaudier setting. Ironically, I can't even take the reins of my newly upended life. People are watching. Waiting. Once again, I'm at the mercy of the men in my life to make all the bad things disappear.

The catch is that they rarely do. If anything, my problems only seem to multiply.

Left with no other options, I retreat to the navy bedroom and shower in an effort to take my mind off the darker thoughts. I dress in an old cream blouse and a cobalt skirt. I brush my hair and find a case of makeup with blush to dust on my cheeks. Then I scowl at the person I find watching me from the mirror's reflection, and I dare her to do something.

Blake claimed that this was a partnership, not a captive situation. It's time for him to prove it.

With renewed determination, I return to the lower level and hunt the various rooms for one in particular. It doesn't take me long to find it: a study tucked near the back of the suite. Here, he kept the decoration minimal. There's just a desk and a chair flanked by bookshelves filled to the brim with leather tomes. The view, however, is second only to the one in the living room. The waterfront gleams in the glow of early dawn, and hints of sunlight ripple over the water. Rolling hills in the distance create a humanizing backdrop as both a warning and a comfort: Mayfield isn't the end-all-be-all. There is a whole world waiting beyond its boundaries.

I don't know how long I let myself stare before the sound of a door opening and closing snaps me into awareness. I turn just in time to catch a figure stepping over the threshold. He pauses, his gaze flitting in my direction as if he hadn't expected to find me here.

He looks even worse than he did before he left. Exhaustion weighs his features down despite the wary frown his mouth contorts into. "You don't have to go hunting for answers this time, Snow," he says, sounding hoarse, as though he had worn out his throat from shouting. "Let's attempt honesty, for once. Whatever you need, you can ask for it."

"I wasn't snooping," I truthfully admit, running my hands over my skirt. Still, I can't resist testing his claim. *Whatever I need.* While I look at him, only one burning request comes to mind. His eyes are bloodshot, and he doesn't seem to realize how tightly he's clutching the doorknob. Not out of anger, but for balance—he's that damn exhausted. "Where were you?"

He flinches. *Damn.* I can almost hear the thought cross his mind. He didn't stop to consider I'd ask about him.

"I'm glad you're awake," he says, approaching the desk. "There's one matter of business we can get out of the way now. Your terms, in writing, as requested." He opens a drawer and withdraws a folder that he places in front of me.

A quick glance reveals everything we discussed laid out in legal terms. Considering the events of last night, he must have had this drafted by a legal team and delivered all on short notice. The man works fast.

"We can sign to make it legally binding. Or base it on my word. The choice is yours."

I eye that beautiful mouth, which is still sporting a bruise left by Ronan's fist. He doesn't even seem to notice the pain or the nice black eye shaping up on the left side of his face. Settling on an option takes mere seconds.

"Give me a pen."

Without a word, he fishes one from his desk and hands it to me. I sign my name on the last page of the documents, and he does the same. Begrudgingly, it seems. Something he said once sticks out to me now. "Honor means nothing to a Hollings."

Even now, he still doubts me.

"I'll have a copy made for you," he assures me before returning the documents to his desk. "And now… I would like you to uphold your other end of our bargain."

"Oh?" I cock my head, wary of the answer.

"Lyle Harlow." He withdraws a cell phone from his pocket and offers it to me. "Call him. Tell him you'll square the debt, no matter the amount. I'll take care of it."

And, later, exact vengeance for every penny? I don't dare question him out loud, but his eyes narrow as if aware of my suspicions.

"You gave me your word," he reminds me. "You put it in writing—"

"I'll do it." I force myself to take the phone, but I can't bring it to my ear just yet.

Blake sighs. "If you want me to, I'll—"

"No." I shake my head. "It's just… I'd like to be alone."

He frowns. I can tell from how the corner of his mouth twitches that he wants nothing more than to refuse. But something in my expression must change his mind, because he turns to the door instead.

"You have five minutes."

I waste the first one trying desperately to catch my breath. Lyle Harlow isn't just a monster looming over my present, but a very real one from my past. Seeking him out before was one thing, but now? Dread forms a pitiful lump in my throat, impossible to swallow down. Not that I have a choice.

Four minutes.

My fingers shake as I punch in the number I know by heart. Surprisingly, the call is answered on the first ring.

"Who is this?" a gruff voice demands.

"I have your money," I croak without giving my name.

A gruff bit of laughter is his response. "Little Snowy Hollings," the man murmurs, lingering over my name. "Most people who don't pay end up having nasty accidents."

God, he sounds too calm. Too…smug.

"Well, I have your money now," I tell him through gritted teeth.

"And you're too late. Someone's already bought your contract, little Hollings."

The world crashes to a halt. My stomach turns, fighting with my heart for supremacy. "W-what?"

"Don't sound so disappointed," Harlow croons sweetly. "We'll be seeing each other soon, Little Hollings. I'll make it worth your while."

He hangs up, and I drop the phone, paralyzed as it slides beneath the desk.

"Snowy?" A fist rattles the door. "What's wrong?"

"N-nothing." I sink to my knees and all but throw myself under the desk, hunting for his phone. I hear the door open, but I can't withdraw. Not with my face on fire and my fear so fucking apparent. *Focus!* I school my expression into a mask as my fingers finally capture the phone. Slowly, I crawl backward on my hands and knees. "Everything is fine…"

I trail off as my gaze falls on Blake's face. His mouth is open, trapped around a question he hasn't voiced. Heavy-lidded eyes shamelessly rake over my bare legs. My skirt rose up without my realizing it, revealing a glimpse of my lace panties.

To his credit, he recovers first, clearing his throat. A coldness washes over his face, displacing any hint of lust. "Is it done? Where should I send the money?"

"The money…" I avert my gaze and rack my brain for an explanation. There isn't one. "He said it's covered," I lie in the end. "Told me to forget about it."

I can almost hear his eyebrow shoot into his hairline.

"Lyle Harlow told you to 'forget' about money owed to him?" Anger lashes from him, as sharp as a whip. "I thought we were past lying."

"We are," I insist, rising to my feet. "And I wasn't. So don't you lie to me." I size him up, surprised to find that he managed to drive some of the exhaustion from his features. He was always so stubborn, refusing to let anything get in his way. Even me. "Where were you?"

Suddenly, he's eyeing the wall beyond my head rather than meeting my gaze directly. "It's not important—"

"That's not what I asked. You were looking for someone," I say, recalling his phone conversation. *Find her!* "A woman. Masha?"

"There are some things that I can't—" He breaks off and exhales sharply. When I look over, he's watching me, his face carefully blank. "I've spent years being alone," he admits. "Fucking no one. Talking to no one. Being no one. Trusting no one. In one night, I learn that most of that pain was based on a lie. Just…just give me some time, but I promise you…"

He's closer in an instant, guiding my chin into his palm. I shiver at the contact. He's so damn warm. So real. In the rare moments he's like this—open—it steals my breath away. It's unfair; my heart can't guard against him.

"I promise you, I'll try to…be different than before," he says, gazing deep into my eyes. "I'll tell you everything.

Anything. But I'm going to need some time."

"And so do I." I step away from him, making sure that no malice seeps into the action. Maybe just fear. My heart races as I remember his request from last night. Fulfilling it. What did it mean? Apparently nothing. He seems even more standoffish than before, even as he taunts me with... what? Trust? "Maybe we should spend some time apart—"

"No." He grabs my hand, squeezing it tight. "Let me take you to lunch."

"I don't think that's a good idea." I muster up what I hope passes for a playful smile while I gently pull my fingers from his. "What if Hunter shows up this time and blackens your other eye?"

Rather than laugh, he...flinches? Something distorts his blank expression, gone in an instant. Alarm?

I choke out a nervous chuckle. "I mean, it's not like you wanted that to happen or anything..."

My joke shouldn't have made an impact at all. No one would be so cunning—stage a beautiful dinner to give the appearance of a relationship—when his real goal all along was far more sinister.

Draw out Ronan. Cause a scene. Force me to choose between him and my brother.

It's such a sick, twisted thought. And when he stiffens, I know the awful truth.

"You *wanted* it to happen, didn't you?" Disgust makes my voice shake, but he doesn't even blink.

"And if I did?"

"You wouldn't…" Pain claws through my chest and I'm forced to brace one hand against the desk, clutching at the fabric over my heart with the other. The answer is clear in his silence: yes, he would. "So was this all just an act, then?" My throat tightens, choking my voice. "Why?"

"How could I trust you?" He sounds so damn calm. Composed. "You run from me at the gala. You scream at me at the Haven event. You accuse me of abuse. And I'm supposed to believe you'll willingly let me touch you in public? Hold you? Don't be so naïve, Snow. I needed you to trust me again—"

"Naïve?" God, he makes that word sound like some magic spell that excuses his actions. Maybe I am. For one brief second, I actually thought we could…

What? Start over?

Fighting back moisture building behind my eyes, I change tack. "You want me to trust you, but then you lie to me…" Damn it. I'm crying. Tears fall hard, and I taste salt as I attempt to swipe them away.

Warmth grazes my chin. His finger?

"Don't fucking touch me!" I stagger to the opposite end of the room, ensuring that a leather armchair stays between us. "How could you plan something so sick? It's almost like…"

Then a sudden suspicion creeps into my thoughts. No. He wouldn't go that far…would he? As insane as it sounds, I have to voice the accusation out loud. "It's almost like *you* released the recordings."

He's so blank. His mouth doesn't even twitch.

And once again, I've hit on the truth.

"No." I shake my head. "God, tell me you didn't."

His gaze fixates on the wall beyond my head. "What else was I supposed to do, Snow? We weren't exactly on speaking terms. You wouldn't even look at me—"

"Because you disgust me!" I can't catch my breath. Can't breathe. The need for fresh air drives me toward the door, but he steps forward, blocking my path.

"Don't do this," he warns, his tone hardening. "Please. We've made more progress in one damn night than we ever could have if—"

"Progress?" I choke out a laugh, and I don't even recognize the high-pitched trill. "You call lying to me and making my brother look like a fool progress? You can forget about whatever you think you've won. There's no way in hell you could convince me to stay in the same room as you."

Something cold settles in his gaze, turning indigo to ice. "Unfortunately, that's an impossible request. As you yourself suggested, we just put it in writing."

And, now, I know what goal he was after all along: I've fallen into his trap. "You unimaginable bastard."

He has the nerve to frown as if insulted. "I gave you every stipulation you required."

"Damn you! And if I refuse now, what? Will you kick my brothers off the board and steal the rug out from under me all over again?" I don't even need to see his face to know the answer: He would. He will. "Go to hell."

"Snow!"

His hand brushes my forearm, but I shove my way past him, racing for the entrance to the suite. I reach the elevator unmolested and slam the call button for the elevator until the doors finally part. I rush inside, and when I turn, I find him watching me from the mouth of the hall. Shadow encases half of his face, rendering his expression unreadable. Not that I need to see it to decipher him.

"Don't bother wasting your breath on your threats," I spit at him, grasping at the wall for balance as the doors shut. I don't sound confident in the slightest, and I hate that he'll get to relish breaking me for a second time. "Don't remind me of what I promised you. Do to those fucking papers what you did to my house: Burn them!"

Ding!

The elevator descends, and I suspect I have roughly a minute before he'll come after me. Men like Blake Lorenz are wolves; rarely do they let their chosen prey escape. Especially not when the damned soul's already bleeding. Somehow, I manage to make it out of the parking garage on my own, which leaves me on a busy city avenue with no sense of direction.

By fate or by chance, I flag a cab down and have the driver take me straight to the hotel. Curious looks follow me as I race inside and head up to the suite Ronan rented. He must have had the staff looking for me, because he's already in the hall, grabbing me the moment I step off the elevator.

I wait for the insults. The shouting. The lectures. But all he does is take one look at my face and pulls me into his arms, no questions asked. And I can't stop myself from sobbing openly, clinging to his chest with my face buried in the fabric of his shirt. He hasn't changed from the suit he was wearing last night, and going off the dampness on his shirt, he was out all night, hunting for me on foot. Because he loves me.

He may not be perfect, but he'd never manipulate my emotions on a sick whim.

Though he will try to protect me from them.

I draw back from him, raising a hand to shield the worst of my bloodshot eyes from his gaze. "I need to know everything you kept from me," I stammer, knowing that I sound insane. Incoherent. Desperate. "Please." I brace my hand on his jaw when he turns away. "Messages? Letters?"

His jaw clenches in reluctant confirmation.

"Then give them to me. Please. I need to read them. I...I need to burn them."

EIGHT

RONAN LEAVES me alone on the floor of my room with an old shoebox. It must have contained one of his newer purchases for me—piles of which litter my room.

Brushing the emotion churning in my stomach aside, I wrench the lid off.

And my heart is assaulted for a second time.

The damn thing is filled to the brim with envelopes, each one heavy with its own unfathomable burden. Each one from Blake Lorenz—all of them but one. Ronan must have shuffled it into the mix without meaning to, a letter directed to all of us: the Hollinges. It's from the lawyer who managed our trust, and bile seeps up my throat as I wrench it open and flip through the contents.

Dear God. It's a summary of outstanding bills as well as a statement acknowledging the loss of the house and our assets. So, so much gone in just a few days. Because of me and my once-impending marriage to Daniel Ellingston. I let him ruin the Hollings name.

And the worst part?

I'm not even a goddamn Hollings.

My skin chills at the thought. I think it's the first time I ever let myself admit it, even inside my head. I, Snowy Gale, am not a Hollings. After twenty-four years of brainwashing and striving to protect the family name, I've never felt hollower without that heritage than I ever felt in Papa's shadow. Would Daniel have even wanted me if he knew who I really am? A half-Lloyd bastard, my mother's dirty little secret?

Mulling over the answer isn't worth the effort.

But it does give me one slim, pathetic, childish bit of hope at how I can help fix this mess for Ronan and Hunter. Clutching the letter to my chest, I hunt for a leather bag and shove the documents into it. After a moment's hesitation, I stow Blake's letters inside it as well. Then I enter the hallway, knowing I'm in for a fight when Ronan comes to block my path.

"Please," he says, eyeing my bag, his expression strained. "I can't take this."

"I know. I'm sorry—"

"Are you? You want to know all the shit I've kept from you just to keep you from getting worse? The messages that bastard left for you? The police haven't done a goddamn thing, and you just waltz out to dinner with the motherfucker?"

"What are you talking about?"

"Forget it." His expression draws tight, closing against me.

All I can do is shake my head and push past him, knowing he won't touch me. "I'll make this right," I swear as I fumble to get the door open. "I promise. I promise I will."

He lets me go, but I know better than to leave through the main entrance. I slip out through a side door instead and walk the entire way to the James Baylor law offices uptown. Inside the lobby, a receptionist wrinkles her mouth at my outfit. She directs me without comment, and I enter an office at the very back of the building, where James Baylor himself is seated behind a mahogany desk.

"Ms. Hollings." He warily shuffles the documents before him and places them aside. "To what do I owe this visit?"

"How bad is it?"

He wrinkles his nose, jolting the wire-rimmed glasses resting on his nose. "I'm not sure I understand what you mean, Ms. Hollings—"

"Our finances," I clarify, more harshly than I intended. "Please don't lie to me. How bad?"

"Ronan's medical bills are outstanding," the man says with brusque efficiency. "There are the back taxes on the property to contend with, not to mention your family's current expenses."

Like the expensive clothing and hotel suites.

"All of it totals in excess of thousands," Baylor finishes. "Hundreds of thousands."

"B-but what if I can fix it?" My fingers shake as I fish the letter from my bag and place it on the desk. "You can start by telling me that none of this matters. Not if... Not if I'm really not a Hollings."

AFTER WHAT FEELS LIKE HOURS, James's secretary enters to place a steaming mug of tea before me. Just as quickly, she's gone, and I feel no closer to an ounce of hope.

"So you're saying there's nothing that can be done?"

Mr. Baylor slowly shakes his head. "I'm afraid not."

I pinch my wrist in exasperation—a childish, last-ditch effort to ensure that this all isn't some insane nightmare. But I don't wake up, and there's no reprieve from the dread building in my veins. "Not even if I took a blood test? Had my siblings disown me?"

"I'm afraid there's nothing that can be done about the business," Mr. Baylor admits, his tone grave. "However..." A curious expression flits over his weathered features. Amusement? Shock? He stands and approaches a wooden cabinet on the other end of the room before I can decipher it. "You are your mother's daughter, after all," he murmurs, though I'm not entirely sure if he's speaking to me.

"Sir?"

"You must understand: She instructed me to only reveal this information if you were either married, to have a child, or if you broached the topic yourself. She had it expressed in writing."

"What are you talking about?"

He rummages through a stack of files and emerges with a black folder in hand. Frowning, he hands it to me. "She had me make the arrangements shortly before she died. From Harrison Lloyd—accounts he'd transferred to her long before his conviction."

Numb, I peer at the pages within the file. Stocks. Bank statements. Businesses. All quietly transferred to Elizabeth Hollings throughout nearly fourteen years—right before Harrison Lloyd's downfall.

"It's all yours," Mr. Baylor explains at the exact moment I realize the staggering sum of the combined estate.

"Th-this can't be right?"

"Twelve million dollars. It may seem redundant," Mr. Baylor remarks, "but congratulations, Ms. Hollings. You are a very wealthy woman. Though…there is one catch."

Dazed, I look up and find him shuffling a stack of documents. "What is it?"

"If I were to give you this money now, it could technically be caught up with the rest of your family's estate."

"Oh?" I swallow hard.

"But," he adds, glancing warily at the door. "Far be it from me to suggest anything nefarious, of course. But if you were to find some other way for the money to get into your hands, I could make the arrangements…"

"Like fraud?" I cringe from the thought. Hunter may have been driven to follow Papa's tactics, but I refuse to.

"No," the man says quickly. "Of course not. Think of it as careful accounting."

"And if I were to do that…how would I?"

Mr. Baylor shrugs. "Any way that would see you legitimately receive the funds from another source."

"And then I could use it?" My mind spins with what such a sum could solve. My debt with Harlow. Ronan's hospital bills. Our running tab at the hotel.

"As far as I'm concerned, Ms. Hollings, there would be nothing preventing you from doing so," Mr. Baylor says. "Nothing at all."

Nothing but finding someone willing to give me twelve million dollars under the pretense of free will. Considering my family's reputation and looming scandal…

Well, it sounds easy enough.

NINE

BLAKE

BROKEN GLASS CRUNCHES UNDERFOOT, but I'm already grasping for the next thing to throw. A lamp this time. It strikes the door frame with a violent thud, ripping a chunk of wood from it in the process.

Damn.

Damn.

Damn it!

I'm sorry. How hard would it be to fucking say?

I pretend like I don't know the answer: *impossible.* A romantic sap from a fairytale could declare as much and all would be well. The princess would be his again. Happily fucking after.

But not me. I've been the villain of the story from the start and nothing I do now could erase the past. The things I've done. To her. For her.

If she knew them all she'd do more than run.

She'd fall—like Humpty Dumpty in that fucking story we once made our own—shattered to pieces. Nothing could ever put them together again.

Not all the king's men.

Not all the king's horses.

And as pathetic as it makes me feel, and as much as I swore to never give that woman power over me again…

I'd rather die than watch that happen.

If only death was anything but final when it came to Snowy Hollings. I've been relegated to the shadows once because of her, forced to watch from a distance as she lived on without me. And now?

I'm too fucking close.

Besides, it's not like she has anywhere left to run. I've already covered every base on the gameboard. Checkmate.

I exhale sharply, reminding myself of that point—my ace in the hole. She's as good as a caged bird. It's only a matter of time before she realizes that.

Maybe if I tell myself that lie enough times, I'll finally fucking believe it.

* * *

SNOWY

I WANDER the streets beyond the law offices for what feels like hours before an impulse I can't name drives me into a cab. When the driver asks my destination, I rattle off one address merely out of habit. It's only as the cab finally reaches the crest of a familiar hill on the outskirts of Mayfield that I realize my blunder.

Hollings Manor is a smoldering, decrepit ruin that looks like a stain on the otherwise pristine landscape. As I step from the cab, I can still smell the smoke. Still see the flames licking at the unfeeling sky.

I still feel that pain.

And I hate him for doing this to me. This twisted, broken landscape is the only haven I have left. The overgrown and neglected weeds offer no solace as I wander toward the back of the property, desperate to reconcile my entire upbringing with what I know now.

Did it kill my mother every day, having to look at me and lie?

Or having to see Brandt, a constant reminder of the man whose bed she crawled into every night?

From what I remember, Harrison Lloyd was a cold, unfeeling man, yet he left me, his bastard, more of a legacy than the boy he'd raised as his son for seventeen years. I doubt Brandt had any heartwarming stories of the man to tell. Our dirty little secret was that he spent so much time with me to avoid having to enter his home for as long as he could. If his father wasn't berating him for some stupid slight, then he was hitting him.

Everyone knew of the abuse, but no one said anything. They smiled, and invited the Lloyds over for brunch, and ignored the black eye their son would occasionally sport.

It was the Mayfield way.

But I saw him—so beautiful, so sweet. I saw his desperate struggle to avoid hate. He never wanted to become Harrison. He never wanted to resemble the man he called Father.

And my mother, as charming as she was, must have loved such a disturbed man. After all, she died for him.

I blink, noticing my surroundings for the first time. I'm nearing the lake, stumbling down the beaten path. Tears stream down my cheeks, a hateful reminder of how much like Elizabeth I am. I'm pathetic. Manipulative. Violence and hate must be hereditary aphrodisiacs, because whenever I think of Blake Lorenz, and the awful things he's done to my body…

I don't feel disgust—not like how I should. No matter how badly he treated me, my body sure had no problem orgasming against him. On him. The vulgar memories set my cheeks on fire, and I start to run, aiming for the only refuge in sight.

The boathouse door is locked. I have to force a window open and climb through it. Inside, I find that Blake Lorenz left his exercise equipment behind. Along with something else thrown in the middle of the space as if in afterthought. My heart races as I approach the small object and sink to the floor beside it.

I brush a trembling finger over the cover of a leather-bound book and it doesn't disappear. A heartbeat later, I clutch it to me with everything I have, and the tears fall faster. The worn copy of *Humpty Dumpty* is all I have left, and I imbibe its pages with a million tears and unsuppressed pain. I bleed into the tiny, remaining sliver of Brandt Lloyd, and I know in my soul that I'd eagerly trade away all of Mama's money just to hold on to this moment forever.

Far too soon, the thud of approaching footsteps shatters it. Gasping, I lurch to my feet. Hiding is my first instinct, and I eye one of the old bookshelves in the corner. Then rage sets in, squaring my shoulders and flooding my limbs with reckless energy. Facing the door, I march toward it and throw it open.

"Just stay the hell away from me!"

"I'm so sorry," a woman remarks, her voice a dreamy murmur. "I just… It was such a beautiful house."

Huh? I fixate my gaze on a figure tiptoeing along the edge of the dock, her arms outstretched. Her bare toes stand out in harsh contrast to the gray wood. Around her legs flutters a thin, white nightgown. It and a curtain of wavy, blond curls are her only protection from the biting chill in the air.

Looking up, she notices me, but her eyes are too wide, her pupils unfocused.

"It's you," she says softly, swaying dangerously close to the water. "You're really here. I'm sorry for trespassing, but maybe... You can tell me what it's like."

I blink as recognition conjures a name to my tongue. "Masha?" She seems no less beautiful and young than she did the first night I saw her. But something is wrong. Alarm prickles down my spine and I start toward her, fighting to keep my expression blank. "What are you doing here?" I glance around but don't see Blake—or anyone else for that matter. Did she walk all this way alone? "Are you okay?"

She smiles, but I've never seen a sadder, more forlorn expression. "Is the water too cold?" she asks, turning her gaze toward it. "God, I just hope it isn't cold."

She turns on her heels, as lithe as a dancer, putting her back toward the lake. A sad tilt of her lips is her best attempt at another charming grin. Then she falls.

"No!" Adrenaline surges. Somehow, I fling my heels aside and dive into the water blind. Ignoring the stinging sensation, I open my eyes and strain through the gloomy, dank waters. Sunlight plays over a pale, sinking shape and I swim toward it, grasping, pulling.

I'll never understand how I manage to drag her onshore, gasping and dazed but still breathing. Then I find my cell phone inside my purse, discarded near the dock, and without loosening my grip on Masha's slender body, I call 911.

* * *

MASHA DOESN'T SAY a word during the ten-minute wait for the ambulance. She merely stares up at the sky, her hair a golden tangle beneath her. As the sirens wail in the background, she giggles brokenly. Then tears form in her eyes and roll down her cheeks. By the time the paramedics usher her onto a stretcher, she's sobbing.

While I watch her, my heart breaks. I wish I could pity her. Feel sorry for her.

But all I see in her pathetic, shivering form…is myself.

"Snowy!"

I'm grabbed from behind and whirled around to face a man I almost don't recognize at first. Blake Lorenz looks haggard in a way I've never seen a man look—not even Ronan. My brother always appeared fragile when distraught. Blake radiates fury and pain, seeming ten times larger and more dangerous than any predator.

"What the hell happened?" He's shaking me, I realize as my head is jostled back and forth. He grips my arms so tightly that his knuckles whiten. With his teeth pulled back from his upper lip, he looks crazed, and if I doubted that he had a soul in his twisted, broken being, then I'm proven wrong. It belongs solely to Masha.

"She fell into the lake," I whisper. The moment he stiffens, I suspect that Blake knows damn well Masha didn't simply "fall."

"Mother of God." He releases me so suddenly that I stumble and have to throw my arms out for balance. He races to Masha, who watches him, shivering on a stretcher as paramedics escort her toward the front of the property, where the ambulance must be parked.

He murmurs something to her in what I assume is German. She answers him tiredly, her voice cracking.

"I'm sorry," she says in English. "I'm so, so sorry."

Her words are swallowed by the wind as she's hustled up the path. Blake lunges on the tips of his toes as if intending to follow. At the last minute, he turns to me. One look at my shuddering frame and he strips his suit jacket before draping it around my shoulders.

"You jumped in after her," he croaks, fingering my damp hair. "You saved her—"

"I didn't do it for you." Only God knows where the vitriol comes from.

How is it possible to hate him now, even as he grapples with his sister's distress? Maybe it's loathing directed solely inward, because a part of me wants nothing more than to hold him, and press him for answers, and offer support. I want to know the truth about Masha, which he seems so desperate to hide. I want to know more about him.

But, even now, his expression forms a door, cutting me off from any hint of emotion. "Thank you anyway," he rasps, taking a step back.

And if I were a good woman, I'd let it end here. I'd hold my barbs for another time. I wouldn't want so badly to kick him while he's down, showing him more courtesy than he's ever shown me. But, deep down, I'm just a vengeful sinner.

Like mother, like daughter.

"You can take those documents and you can rip them to shreds," I tell him, hating how breathless I sound.

He's stoic once more, but I'm the one sobbing openly, huddling beneath his warmth even though I want nothing more than to shrug it off. I try, but my fingers won't release the tailored cotton. When gestures fail me, my words are the only weapon I have left.

"I changed my mind. Forget our agreement. It's over."

His jaw clenches, a subtle warning. "I suggest you think carefully—"

"Or what? You'll throw my brothers off the board out of spite? Rescind your offer of assistance?" I don't even need to see the stubborn tilt of his jaw to know the truth. Harrison may not be his biological father, but the man trained him well. He's just as heartless. Just as cold. And I'll treat him the same way my mother did Harrison: like a glorified bank. "Do it. I've decided that I don't need nor do I want your help."

"Oh?" His eyes narrow and I can't ignore how my breath stalls in my chest. "And what the hell do you intend to do?"

I push past him and start toward the path with my head held high, even as my heart turns to stone. "I'll do what I should have done before I ever signed my life away to you."

He inhales sharply, a growl-like sound that stops me dead in my tracks. "You don't mean to…" He sounds doubtful. As if I wouldn't be that stupid. That spiteful.

"Why not?" I can't bring myself to face him. I glare at the trees in front of me instead. So much land tied to a single family's name. Forrest would die to know what's become of his goddamn legacy. If I were to thank Blake for one damn thing, it would be for finally severing any ties I had to it. "Maybe I'll let you have a front-row seat."

The idea forming in my head is too childish to ever enact. So devious. Perhaps only someone as demented as he is would ever propose it. Fittingly, he doesn't even need a further hint to guess my intent.

"No." He advances, and before I can move, my forearm is in his grip. "Hell no. *Fuck* no. I won't let you near it. Do you hear me?"

"Oh yes!" I wrench away from him, but he doesn't relent. Neither do I. I twist and tug until my arm strains in its socket, which draws a cry from my lips.

Finally, he lets me go, and I race up the path. When I'm a safe distance away, I turn for one last quip.

"If you want to play your sick games, I won't be a participant. I'll find another man to make me his toy," I snarl. "Anyone but you."

"Snow…" His eyes practically glow in the faded daylight, more monstrous than human. "Don't. You don't fucking mean it."

I manage to smile, even as tears continue to fall and my legs buckle beneath me. "I do. See you at Bolles. I'd rather auction myself in a room full of strangers than ever trust you again."

Then I turn, leaving him there.

And I run.

TEN

WITH THE HOTEL out of the question and no other refuge in mind, I'm once again forced to rely on pure impulse. Maybe it's the thought of Masha, so pale and innocent, that drives me toward her polar opposite.

"Snowy?" Sloane looks at me like I'm a three-headed demon cursed to darken her ornate doorstep.

I'm standing in the foyer of the Sebastián mansion, clutching a leather handbag to my chest, my clothing drenched and worthless, my eyes bloodshot. Honestly, I don't know what to expect. A warm welcome? A cold shoulder?

Suddenly, the Spanish beauty snaps her fingers to summon a maid. "Hot tea," she demands. "And call my manicurist." She eyes my cracked, worn nails with a frown. Gently, she takes my hand, tugging me inside and toward the winding staircase. "It's about time we had the chance to properly catch up."

Two hours later, I'm bundled in a robe, lounging on a chaise in the upstairs spa of the Sebastián home. Sloane is sprawled on a chair beside me, a mug of tea in her freshly manicured hand. A frown tugs at her mouth, and she lowers her gaze while flicking an imaginary piece of lint from her lap.

"I tried to call, you know? When you didn't return it, I thought… Everything got so insane."

"I know," I say.

Sloane, on a good day, was my friend only in the most superficial of terms. Being seen on my arm got her exposure, and I let her screw my fiancé in secret. Everyone won. Until now. I don't find Daniel lurking in this posh suite, and Sloane seems determined to avoid mentioning him by name—along with any other men rumored to be in my orbit.

"You can bring up the headlines," I blurt. "I won't be upset. It's all lies."

"Really?" Sloane raises an eyebrow, her lips pursed as if to trap a multitude of questions behind them. In the end, she settles on one. "Is he really as bad as they say?"

All I can do is shake my head.

Sloane sighs. "Good. But I'll make sure Daddy doesn't invite him to any future galas—"

"You don't have to do that," I say. "There's nothing between us."

"Like you and Daniel?" Sloane prods.

I glance at her sharply. "What do you mean?"

"You dated him for nearly two years, and in an instant, it's all over." She sounds more wistful than I'd like.

"Well, he did singlehandedly cause my family's ruin," I remind.

"I didn't mean it like that." Sloane bites her lower lip, parting her thick hair with her fingers. "I just mean... He loved you, you know. He really did."

I mull over that statement. Somehow, I don't bring myself to mention the obvious catch to his so-called love—their dalliances behind my back, for instance.

"Just admit it," Sloane adds before I can respond at all. "If you could go back, before everything happened. You would, wouldn't you?"

Would I? I turn away, eyeing the view of the Sebastiáns' estate from a nearby window. It's a far cry from the bustling city landscape glimpsed from Blake's penthouse. Here, the neat gardens and fountains create a carefully crafted fantasy, like the backdrop of a gilded cage.

"I don't know..."

"So that's a yes, then," Sloane counters, her tone cold. "Bad investments aside, at least Daniel never wound up in the tabloids under the guise of assaulting you."

"I don't want to fight," I admit. Instead, I draw my knees to my chest, admiring my neatly trimmed toes with pale-pink nails. "If it makes you feel any better, I need a favor."

"Oh?" She faces me, suddenly animated. "Money? References? A tabloid contact?"

She practically squeals at the possibilities. Apparently, her life has been boring without being caught in the whirlwind that is the Hollings rumor mill.

"No." I draw in a breath and release it with a harsh sigh. "You know men. Like…like the kind who belong to my father's club?"

A perfectly trimmed black eyebrow shoots into a fringe of black hair. "*Que*? Oh, Snowy, you aren't that girl. Those men… It's not like you think."

Her serious tone makes me wonder just what experience she has with Bolles men. But I've tangled with the worst of them all.

"It's not like that. I need you to contact one of them to arrange something."

"Oh?" She leans in, drowning me beneath the sweet scent of her perfume. "Like what?"

"An auction," I blurt, and her eyes widen. "But it's not what you think. And I need your help to ensure that it goes exactly how I need it to."

Riling Blake aside, an auction could have a much more practical purpose. Securing my mother's money, for one.

Mr. Baylor claimed that, as long as a transaction was legitimate, it would be legal. He never mentioned whether said agreement couldn't be scandalous...

"I'm listening," Sloane says, her expression wary. "Okay. Tell me what you need me to do."

Hours later, my plan sounds less insane, at least on paper. In fact, arranging to auction off a woman's body is surprisingly like arranging an engagement party. There are guests to invite and outfits to plan. At least in this case, the venue is already secure. Through Sloane and her wealth of masculine contacts, I have an in at Bolles.

More importantly, I have a date.

Tomorrow night.

* * *

"ARE YOU SURE ABOUT THIS?" Sloane asks from beyond the door of her private en suite bathroom. Her concern seems genuine—the most authentic emotion I've ever witnessed her express. Perhaps she's right to be. I told her only as much as I had to.

One, that I needed to arrange an auction at Bolles on short notice.

Two, that I needed a man to secretly bid on my behalf, with a limit I specified.

"For what it's worth, I'd trust Andrew with my life," Sloane adds. "He's gay. He only joined Bolles because his father is a homophobic *puta* and the membership keeps him off his back."

She's trying to assure me, but I doubt anything can. I'm insane. Any woman would have to be to recklessly throw herself into the fire with only a thin lifeline as protection. Reckless or scorned. Hell hath no fury, after all, and I've been bathed by the flames too many times to fear them now.

"I...I think I'm ready."

Sloane opens the door and gasps at my appearance. Rather than risk crossing my brothers to fetch a gown from home, I was forced to raid Sloane's private collection. Where my wardrobe was designed to sparkle and shine, her gowns were composed with another goal in mind entirely.

"You look like sex," she says, nodding appreciatively.

I agree with her. Wearing a skintight black gown that hugs my nonexistent curves, I look like sex as Blake Lorenz taught me. Dirty, brutal fucking. A screen of lace covers my breasts, and only a strategic placement of the design shields my nipples from view. Two waist-high slits on either side render the skirt little more than an ineffective dangling bit of silk. With my hair wrangled by Sloane's stylist into a tight knot at the nape of my neck, there are no wayward curls to shield my face from view. Or the fierce expression I barely recognize, enhanced by burgundy lipstick and eyes lined in kohl.

Tonight, I intend to take my life back from Blake Lorenz—no matter what it costs me.

"You look…terrifying," Sloane amends, though a bit of sadness seeped into her tone.

I look over and find her frowning. She doesn't recognize this new woman, either. Whether that's a good thing or bad, I've yet to decide.

"I need one last favor," I start after one last glance at myself in the mirror.

"Already ahead of you," she says. "Do you want to take the limo or the Rolls?"

BOLLES WELCOMES me like an old friend. The strained, unhealthy kind with no warmth lost between meetings. How Papa used to taunt me with it, using it like the cruelest punishment, even the night he assaulted me.

Desperate girls spread their legs in Bolles.

Angry, bitter, jaded ones, however? We bare our legs proudly in couture and stroll into the club with our chins jutting into the air. Nothing can reach me through the impenetrable shield hate has formed around my heart. Not the lingering, lustful glances cast my way or the curious, amused ones by the few hostesses already demeaning themselves for the members of this establishment.

Inside, I head directly for the foyer and into the spacious lounge on the bottom level. Chandeliers cast a seductive, soft glow over the inhabitants: men in suits and girls in skimpier attire than mine. They eye me like a new toy placed on the shelf of an exclusive store.

One of them, a smirking blond with his shirt unbuttoned to reveal a muscular chest, approaches me. "I'm Andrew," he says, eyeing me up and down. "Sloane told me all about you."

For a split second, doubt creeps in as his gaze rakes over my breasts. Before I stiffen fully, he winks.

"This way. The arrangements have already been made."

He leads me past the billiard room, into an even wider area. At first appraisal, it resembles a lounge of some kind, with a round platform in the center surrounded by black leather chairs. A silvery spotlight adds a mysterious atmosphere, only enhanced by the dark-blue walls and polished marble floors. Men are already seated, facing what I'm beginning to suspect is a stage. Dressed in expensive suits, they're watching. Waiting.

For the first time, real alarm sinks into my veins, fighting with determination for potency. Do I really intend to demean myself just to make a point? With one glance at the few empty chairs—and the one man missing from this crowd—I have my answer.

Hell fucking yes.

"Don't worry."

I jump as a hand presses against my lower back, but it's only Andrew, gently guiding me forward.

"You're the last…guest of the evening," he assures me. "I'm sure you'll fetch an interesting price."

This must be an event they regularly hold here, I realize. Lingering on the outskirts of the room are other women dressed no less shamelessly. Have all of them been bought and sold already? Disgraced heiresses? Desperate waitresses? Women looking for a thrill, as Sloane admitted to me?

I can't find the pride to pity any of them as I approach the raised platform. There's no announcer there to add pomp and circumstance. No thrilling music to count the seconds down. The moment I brace a heel against the dais, a man calls out, "Five hundred."

"Eight hundred," another says, his casual tone suggesting he just bid on a pair of shoes or piece of jewelry, not a woman.

"A thousand," someone adds to the chorus of bids.

For a painful second, there's no other offer. "Two thousand," someone calls finally— Andrew, perched on a chair in the back. Catching my relieved glance, he nods. "Five thousand," he adds after another man has countered his offer.

Minutes pass, and it almost feels like a strange, thrilling game. One played after too much wine at some rich bastard's soirée. A game of "who can be the biggest show off" by throwing unseemly amounts of money around.

"Six thousand," bids another man, his face obscured by the glow of the spotlight.

There's a moment's pause. Then I hear Andrew wager. "Seven thousand—"

"Ten thousand." A newer voice cuts through the fray and any innocence this event may have held is promptly shattered. The devil enters the room, looking as though he crawled his way from hell. His suit is rumpled, his hair a wild mess. Cold, glaring eyes find me, cutting through every obstacle in his way. "Twenty thousand," he adds before another man can even finish voicing his bid.

A shudder runs through the room. Heads turn, eyeing the newcomer curiously. What was fun and games is now a gladiatorial match, with money as the weapon and my body as the prize.

Andrew, as Sloane insisted, proves to be more reliable than expected. "Thirty," he says, sounding unfazed by this new challenger.

As if shrugging off a fly, Blake flicks a different amount off his tongue. "Fifty."

The confused murmurs grow. Excitement and tension crackle in the air. I'm sweating in my borrowed dress, aware of how my chest heaves with every breath. Sloane warned me to be careful. *That gown is killer, but one wrong move and your goods will be on full display.*

They must be, because, if anything, the only man standing suddenly looks taller. His voice grates, taking on an increased urgency. "One hundred."

"Two," Andrew says without missing a beat.

"One million."

My jaw drops, along with most of the men's jaws in this room. The wildest amount I ever pictured anyone pledging was maybe a few thousand. And, by anyone, I meant the one bastard who thwarted my original plans for an auction. Never in my most dangerous nightmares did I imagine him putting that much of a price on me. Or a bounty.

"Two million." A slender figure rises from the crowd. Andrew, his face suddenly drawn with concentration. "Four," he adds when Blake unflinchingly counters.

The game ends as other men lose interest. It's a two-man race now, each naming an amount more absurd than the last.

Six.

Seven.

Nine.

Ten…

Oh God no. Terror corrupts my limbs, turning bone and blood to cement. The closer the amount creeps to my limit, the harder I sweat. Quake. Tremble.

He can't. He can't really…

No. He won't.

Teeth bared, he snarls, "Fifteen million." Loudly, as if he wants the entire damn world to hear. To know the price he'd pay for the privilege of owning me. Claiming me.

Dread has me in its grasp even before I force myself to glance at Andrew. His teeth are gritted, but the silence stretches on as he heeds my hard limit.

A second passes.

Another.

Sold.

No one says it. I feel it: possession. Wrapping around my throat, yanking me the few steps it takes to descend the dais. He doesn't beckon me or even call me by name. He doesn't have to. As he glowers like a fucking psychopath, his gaze alone warns any other man from glancing in my direction. It's like I no longer exist, a pawn in his possession, unreachable to any other.

I assume the other women purchased within these walls would approach their buyer with a mixture of curiosity and excitement. They'd submit to this creature who bought them like a commodity.

I run.

Panting, I find that Bolles is a maze of dark, winding hallways and hardwood floors. Floors that echo, taunting me with every footfall that lands in my wake. Slow and steady, but never far behind, he chases me into a foyer. Up a polished set of stairs. Farther. Farther. Farther…

Rounding a corner, I nearly run into a woman leaving a bathroom, her arms laden with cleaning supplies. She gives me an odd look as I lunge past her, closing the door. The damn room is too narrow. There are no hiding spaces—just the sliver of space beside the black marble toilet, its basin blue with cleaning fluid.

He doesn't knock. He doesn't even barge inside. The doorknob turns slowly, as if he's savoring the sound of my racing heartbeat. Relishing in the frantic swell.

I stop breathing as he forces his bulk through the doorway. He seems that damn large—he can't merely step inside. He crams every inch of his body into the narrow space. Slowly, he flicks his gaze over me, molten hot, as he reaches up to tug his tie loose.

"Turn around."

My body obeys, a slave to the ragged tone of voice I've never heard him use before. It's volatile, grinding inside me, irritating raw flesh. A warning of what's to come.

"Bend over."

My hands land on the toilet seat, but I choke down any disgust I may feel. It's primal, this compulsion taking control of my spine. I can't resist. Not even as his fingers graze my throat, practically shaking with possession.

"Open your mouth."

The moment I do, silk is shoved between my lips. His tie. His thumb strokes my jaw until I bite down, muffling any sound I might make.

"You think I'll let them fucking hear you?" he murmurs into my ear. There's a terrifying calmness in his voice, far beyond rage, or anger, or even hate. It's acceptance.

We'll only ever belong together like this. Fit together like this: two halves of the same broken puzzle piece. "Hell no."

Two fingers delve beneath my skirt and find the panel of my thong. "You think I'd let them get a fucking taste of what is *mine?*"

God. My eyelids flutter as he rubs between my folds, easing me open. Warm wetness greets him, and he takes advantage, painting heated flesh with the proof of my arousal.

He growls. I hear his zipper come undone, and a heartbeat later, I'm thrown forward as he plunges inside me. My knees buckle. My arms strain to support my weight as my face is brought ever closer to the water glistening in the toilet.

But he doesn't fuck me.

He breaks me open, grinding every inch of himself he can fit into the cracks. I cry out, muzzled by the makeshift gag. I'm mute to every thrust and groan. No one can hear me whimper. Moan. Scream.

"No fucking way." He never stops speaking to me, listing every transgression committed against him. "I saw them. Looking at you. Fucking you with their eyes. But you're mine—" He bucks his hips, and my arms give out. My chin hits the toilet seat, leaving my ass in the air, my body at his mercy. "Fuck. I should string you up. Never let you out of my fucking sight. Fuck. Fuck!"

He doesn't even give himself the chance to experience his release in full. He pulls out, still impossibly hard. Dazed, I watch him stuff himself into his pants, his face a mask of pure insanity.

"Car," he says simply. "Five minutes."

He strips his coat and tosses it over my heaving frame before storming into the hall.

Five minutes.

ELEVEN

I LEAVE Bolles a captive after entering just a moment earlier with my soul in play. I wagered and badly lost. My tormentor is waiting for me out front, ready and willing to usher me into his dark chariot. Not that he needs it. He'll drag me into Hades with him if he must. By the aid of a vehicle. By my hair.

"In," he grunts, stepping aside to wrench the door to the back seat open.

I move past him, numb. Dazed. As he slams the door behind me, I realize he drove here himself. Radiating tension, he climbs into the driver's seat. A telltale click betrays that the locks engage, trapping me within.

We return to his suite in silence, crowding into the elevator wordlessly. The moment the doors part on the top floor, he commands me forward with a curt nod, his gaze unreadable. With my shoulders squared, I enter the foyer.

Something heavy rams into me from behind, forcing me

against the nearest wall where a framed portrait of a painted landscape hangs. Fabric tears and cold air rushes to assault my suddenly bare torso.

"Turn," he commands, but he does it himself, shoving me back. Darkness taints the blue of his irises as he grabs my panties with both hands. Tears them off. Throws the lace aside. His cock is already captured in his fist, straining to enter me.

Groaning, he lifts my thigh against his hip and shoves the swollen crown inside me.

My cry cuts the air, loud without anything to stifle it. The sound only makes him harder. Madder. He drives into me, grunting, teeth clenched, eyes pressed shut.

"You're so beautiful." Every praise lands like a curse. "So wet for me. God, so wet. Fucking hell…"

He's ruthless, taking me with reckless need. Like he's drowning. Starving. Dying. Only this can keep him afloat, sustain him, keep him alive. Only this gives his life any damn meaning.

He drags me to the floor, rutting me from behind with my face pressed against the marble. Drool coats my cheeks. I can't suck in enough air to gasp. Moan. I claw at the floor, a mass of tense, clenching, churning muscle and nerves, taking as much of him as I can. So deep that it fucking burns. It bleeds.

"That's right," he urges, sounding crazed, as he pulls out only to seek his way into my body through a different route.

A tighter one that clenches against him. He has to dip into my gaping "cunt" to find enough lubrication. "So goddamn wet. Let me in, Snow. Won't hurt… Let me in… Jesus Christ!"

My head rears back as I find the voice to scream. God, it doesn't hurt—it desolates. He claims me in a way only he can, forcing me to accept him. Need him. Crave every fucking burning, painful, stretching inch.

And inch.

"So fucking good," he mutters into the nape of my neck. "So good. Fucking hell. Feel like heaven. Heaven…"

The intimacy of this way of fucking undoes him too quickly. He groans, collapsing against my back. But he doesn't pull out. I doubt he can, gripped so tightly by my body for every spasming, unbidden release.

"Do you know what you do to me?" he demands, grasping strands of my hair. Pulling on them. "Drive…me… goddamn…insane."

I was wrong. Still hard, he flexes his hips, driving into me for another series of punishing thrusts. Too much. Can't take. Blind. Numb. Dumb.

Burning.

My body goes limp before jolting back to life, enslaved to every grinding, harsh, bruising bit of friction.

"You're mine now," he tells me, thrusting even deeper. Faster. Oh God, too fast. "Mine!"

My vision goes white. I'm weightless, robbed of sensation. Just the knowledge of him crushing down on my spine, his presence inescapable as my body rides every dizzying throe. This isn't an orgasm. It's dying, becoming something twisted and new from the ashes.

"You're fucking mine," he promises, his voice hoarse. "From now on, you're fucking mine."

* * *

I COME to on what feels like a bed. How we got here, I have no clue. I smell him sweating and breathless beside me. My inner thighs throb with his release, my body burning in the aftermath of his possession. Somehow, I know without having to look that he's ready to take me again.

It's like we're two cogs of one of those wind-up toys. He's the crank, twisting into me. I'm the part that jumps across the floor at the whim of every motion.

"Touch yourself." He voices the command into my ear, biting the lobe when I don't comply fast enough.

My fingers rise from the bed, trembling and weak. I guide them down my belly until they meet a mass of swollen, slick flesh.

"Holy hell." He inhales, positioning himself to watch every illicit motion. "More," he grates, his eyes glowing in the dark. "Harder. The way I know you've imagined me touching you."

Like a deranged madman, apparently. Rough. Rigidly. Tentatively slipping inside, just to the nail bed before chickening out.

"No." He leans in closer, inhaling the scent on my skin. His hand captures my wrist and the pressure increases.

My fingers have no choice but to enter me. One. Another. "Oh God—"

"Yes." He bites me again, grinding a ridge of flesh on my throat between his teeth. "Fucking yes."

He guides me in and out, but never deep enough. Hard enough. Fast enough. He coaxes me up that dangerously high peak, but never close to the edge.

"The things you make me do," he admits, barely intelligible. "I've fucked my fist for weeks. Come inside my goddamn pants. You make me so fucking... Fuck."

I stiffen as he forces my thumb against the bundle of nerves aching for the most stimulation. One hard flick has me gasping. After another, I'm grinding my hips against my own damn fingers.

"You were made for me," he declares. "For this. To be fucked by me. Fucking me. You're fucking *for* me."

I squeeze my eyes shut against his expression. Too raw. Too dangerous. I focus on the white-hot flames building inside my belly, growing hotter with every twist. Every thrust. Far too soon, he bats my hand aside. Hot air assaults the throbbing flesh. God no. Then I open my eyes and find him hunched on all fours, his head lowering.

He spears me open with his tongue, fucking me with the stiff tip. I lose my voice from screaming. I lose my fucking mind. I only find pieces of it again: on my knees as he takes me from behind, slamming my shoulder against the headboard.

"Fuck," he growls, his face buried against my neck. "I'd give you anything…everything. I'd give you everything. But I can't… I don't. Trust. Can't trust."

He rears back, spilling himself inside me before I can anticipate the searing warmth. For some reason, that last confession resonates more than the others. *I'd give you everything. Anything.*

"Purse," I croak, too exhausted to lift my body from the twisted sheets. "Purse."

Frowning, he rises from the bed and returns a second later, dropping my handbag beside me. Blindly, I reach inside and grab a letter at random. He eyes it blankly as I press it against his palm.

"Read."

I can't find the words to explain his expression. Maybe there aren't any. Just feelings: an aching clench of my heart and a twist of my belly. Things I hate feeling. Things only he can make me feel.

He leaves again, but he doesn't go far. Into a bathroom, maybe? I hear water running. When he pads back to the bed, soothing warm runs between my legs, cleaning me up. He washes me slowly, using the same rag to stroke my backside and down my thighs. Satisfied, he settles beside me, sitting upright. Paper crinkles, manipulated by his large hands. A man like him isn't the type to write letters or read them. They forge contracts and sign lives away with the stroke of a pen.

"Dear Snow…" He sounds worse than I do. Ragged and hoarse. After clearing his throat, he tries again. "Dear Snow. I don't want to hate you. I can't hate you."

My skin heats, and I roll onto my side, hunting his expression. He keeps his face utterly stoic, hiding himself from me, even now.

"And I should. There are moments where I still look at you and I feel it. I despise you so fucking much. Then others… when the light catches your hair, and your eyes seem so goddamn blue, and all I can fucking think about is being inside you. Near you. And that's the worst part," he insists darkly. "You don't want me to crave you the way I should. Need you the way I fucking need you. If anything, you should ignore me. Run away. Because I'll fucking chase you. I'll chase you until you stop running."

He crumples the page in his fist and tosses it aside.

"My first fifteen-million-dollar fuck," he grumbles as he staggers for the door as if drunk. Looking back, he frowns, the expression almost pitying. "I wish I could say it wasn't worth it. I fucking wish I could."

He leaves, letting the door sway in his wake. I'm too tired to track where he goes. Somewhere far from this room, down the stairs, but still in the suite. Like any predator, he won't leave his kill for long.

Groaning with the effort, I feel along the bed for the letter. My heart lurches when I finally find it, clutching it tightly. I roll onto my stomach and unfurl it, straining my eyes to read in the dark.

I seek out every scribbled word in that scrawl I know so well.

Only to find nothing.

Not on this side. Not on the other.

It's blank.

A sickening feeling runs through me like a lance as I drag my bag closer and grab another letter at random. I rip it open, unfurling the pages. There are three of them, each one blank. So is the next. And the next. And the next.

Every single envelope contains a varying number of blank pages.

And suddenly, I know why: He sent me blank, fake letters, knowing that I'd never read one.

TWELVE

I WAKE up sprawled over a strange bed in a strange, darkened room. Gray walls and hardwood floors form a bare, utilitarian prison. At least at first glance—a second appraisal reveals that the door is open, and faint rays of daylight seep through black curtains, revealing a distinctly masculine air. Steel-colored sheets cover the substantial mattress. The frame is dark wood, with simple, sleek furniture rounding out the drab surroundings: a nightstand in the same style as the bed, a leather chaise near one of the massive windows, and a floor lamp placed beside the door to a walk-in closet. From here, I can make out seemingly endless rows of hanging suits.

A terrible realization strikes: This is his room. His bed.

I scramble to my feet, alarmed to find countless balls of crumpled paper mingled in the sheets. Then I take a step and groan as my body throbs in a million different ways. My back aches. My head pounds. A steady burn builds between my legs—in both the front and the back. My cheeks flame as I remember the myriad of ways Blake Lorenz violated my body.

The ways I *let* him violate me.

Fifteen million dollars wasted on one senseless night.

He must be insane.

Dreading what I'll find, I hunt the floor for my dress but find nothing, not even my panties. Facing him naked isn't even a remote option, so I cut my losses and snatch a white shirt from his color-coded closet. On me, it's long enough to reach my knees, providing enough cover to give me the strength to leave the room. Before I do, I notice another alarming detail: My purse is missing, along with the bank documents stowed inside it.

Insane, yes, but even Blake Lorenz wouldn't be so bold as to brazenly search through my belongings. Right? I feed myself that lie, even as the truth becomes clearer with every step I creep from the bedroom on my way to the upstairs hall. I can sense him radiating frustration and rage from the lower level.

He's standing before his desk, facing the doorway. Shadows beneath his eyes reveal he hasn't slept. In days. Unsurprisingly, my bank documents are spread before him. I suspect he's spent hours poring over every one, reconciling the pure folly of my deception.

"Well played," he says coldly. "The pauper's become a princess again." He snatches up one of the pages and throws it so hard that it slides across the desk. "A very wealthy princess. Tell me, did you intend to milk me for so much or did you get caught up in the moment?"

I flinch at the vitriol flung my way. He's furious, but for once, I don't think it's all directed at me. He glares down at his hands, flexing them against the wood. A fifteen-million-dollar fuck, he mused, according to my hazy memories. Last night, he deemed that amount of money well spent.

"You weren't supposed to win me at all," I say, alarmed to find my voice a rasp. My throat feels rubbed raw. No wonder—he bit it. Stroked it. Coaxed a million dollars' worth of screams from it. "I... You weren't supposed to win."

He frowns at the idea, as if I'd suggested he stop breathing on a whim. "You thought I'd sit there and let some other bastard buy you? Own you? Jesus Christ." He throws his head back for a long, disturbing laugh that never goes beyond the surface. When he meets my gaze again, all I find in his eyes is pain, raw and exposed. "There's no fucking amount I wouldn't pay. I'd scrape together every goddamn cent. You remember that the next time you get the urge to play your little game. Though I suggest you consider the welfare of others first."

I suck in a breath at the thinly veiled threat. I've outed Andrew as my accomplice, and the monster before me didn't miss a damn thing. Suddenly, I know his motive for confronting me like this in the first place: to catch me off guard and learn just who nearly outbid him.

His hands curl into fists over the desk's surface. "Who was he?"

"No one," I croak. He must hear the truth in my voice, because his jaw relaxes by a fraction. "I asked him to help me. That's all—"

"You know I had it all fucking planned," he admits, shaking his head. "How I'd make you stay. Make you earn every fucking cent. I'd lock you away. I'd make you crave my cock as badly as I crave you. I'd make…I'd make you need me."

He sounds deranged. No, even worse. He sounds one hundred percent truthful.

"How?" I find myself asking. "By manipulating me again? By lying?"

He shrugs, his eyes narrowing. "By fucking. It's the only goddamn way you seem to hear me. Listen to me. Understand me. When I'm so deep inside you, there's nothing fucking else."

I turn away, my cheeks flaming. The view from the window offers no reprieve. The water looms below, as gray as the storm clouds rolling in over the horizon. It's as if the entire world is trying to warn me in visual clues: *Run. He's dangerous. He's fucking mad, Snow.*

"And, now, I don't need you anymore," I say, voicing what he seems unwilling to.

"You don't," he admits. "You're a free woman. Congratulations—"

"So, now, maybe you'll stop treating me like a goddamn object and listen to *me* for once!" My fingers knot into fists. I could hit him if I were close enough, and it takes everything I have to stay back. "All I wanted—all I asked— was that you talk to me on equal terms. Trust me. Open up to me! All you've done is lie, and cheat, and steal—"

"You want to talk?" He cuts his gaze toward me, his features contorted by shadow. "Fine. Let's talk. But that's the problem, isn't it? I can't say a fucking word to you that doesn't make me want to bash my fucking skull in. None of it means a goddamn thing. But then all of it means *everything*. I can't feel a fucking shred of anything real unless I'm around you."

He's closer, invading my space without care. His fingers capture one of my curls, grinding it into a wild tangle. I stiffen at the deliberate act, but I can't move. My body won't obey any of the frantic commands my brain issues.

"I want to tell you every-fucking-thing. God, I do…" He swallows hard, his expression constricted, as if something is squeezing him from within, causing unimaginable pain. "But at the same time, I'd rather hurt you. Lie to you. Cheat. Steal from you. I'd rather fucking break you than give you an ounce of myself. Because…because if you turn against me again, there won't be anything left. I won't have a damn thing."

Tears spill from my eyes, impossible to stop. It's the first time he's ever directly addressed his past as Brandt. Without mocking. Without taunting. It's the pain I've feared facing for ten damn years, and my heart is no match for it now.

"I'm sorry—"

"I know." His other hand encircles my throat, tightening just enough to render me silent. "And I want to believe that. I do. But, fuck, I *can't*." He moves, using his bulk to steer me back. Back.

It's a shock when my shoulder blades strike cold, unyielding glass. And the look in his eyes makes me suck in a startled breath—a pained stage between determination and recklessness. The same way he was when he set my home on fire from the inside. The same look he was wearing when he bid for me. When he swore while buried inside me that I was his alone.

"There are times when I look at you and all I see is that girl again," he admits, hissing the words into my hair, his breath igniting the sweat gathering along my scalp. "So sweet. So innocent. And all I fucking want to do is..." His fingers form a fist with a chunk of my curls trapped between them. "Crush her."

"Talk to her," I croak, aware of his touch still pressed against my throat. "Just talk to me. Tell me what you feel. Just talk to me, please."

"Feel?" His mouth flattens into a hard line. It's as if he's never heard the word before—or at least not in so long; he's forgotten its meaning. "All I feel is need. I need you in a way I can't fucking stand. Like I've never needed anything. It drives me fucking insane."

"So talk to me," I murmur, though I don't know how I found the sense to speak. I should run. Every instinct in my body is urging me to—but I can't seem to move an inch. "Keep talking to me. Tell me—"

"I need to let the world know you're mine. I had you first. I will always have you first." His eyes glaze over, unfocused.

Suddenly, I'm spun around, forced face-first against the glass. I turn my head, putting one eye to the view while keeping the other trained solely on him.

He looks beautiful like this. A tempest. A raw, violent thunderstorm about to descend. Groaning, he smooths his hands up my bare thighs. A shudder runs through me, an electric current lacing from his fingertips. The higher he goes, the harsher it feels, until my teeth chatter with the force of it.

"I need to hear you," he adds, sounding dazed, even as his fingers find me without hesitation. "How it feels when I'm inside you so fucking deep." He slides a digit inside me and my lips part on cue.

"Hurts," I whisper. "Like…like you're splitting me open. Every time."

He growls, satisfied with the answer. Another finger slides home to join the first, extending the burn. "It should," he agrees. "Because that's what you do to me, every fucking time. You split me open. You make me into a fucking… fuck. Do you know what you taste like?" He laughs, stretching me from the inside out, drawing a moan with every deliberate stroke. "*Snow*. How fucking pathetic is that? Snowy tastes like snow… But you do." He lunges, encasing me from behind. His pelvis presses against my ass, revealing a teasing brush of the erection stiffening against the front of his slacks. "Pure. Clean. Like fucking snow."

He bats a tangle of hair from my neck and lathes the exposed area with his tongue. A groan escapes my clenched teeth, melding with his weary sigh.

"Like this," he rasps as if struggling to remember something, put it into words. "Only like this. Feel…better. Only like this."

There's no explanation. He removes his hands from me to tug at the front of his pants and yank them down. One hand captures my thigh while his hips buck, guiding his cock between my legs. Inside.

"Talk to me," he begs as he builds a slow, torturous rhythm. "Need you. Talk to me."

"You're breaking me," I tell him, my voice cracking into jagged syllables and panting breaths. "Breaking me."

"Yes." He grasps a fistful of my hair, drawing my face toward his. His lips nudge mine and he licks them open, shameless and ruthless. "And look. The whole fucking world can see it. How good it is when I fuck you. Say it."

"So good." Sensations overwhelm me. I squeeze my eyes shut against them, but he growls, nipping my lower lip. Jawline. Any part of me he can reach.

"You watch," he warns. "Watch what you do to me."

I open my eyes to madness. It consumes his entire being, darkening the hue of his gaze, dragging me down with him.

He swivels his hips, deepening his entry. More. More. Too much. "I'm drowning," he croaks. "So wet. Drowning me. Drowning."

The sounds of slapping flesh dominate. He said that this is the only way we can speak: in frantic, driving motions. Whispered curses. Heat. And sin. And skin on skin. All of it swelters, wrapping me in a terrifying, claustrophobic cocoon of fire, and lust, and Blake.

"Shit, I feel you coming," he gasps out.

And I come undone. Literally. I'm a puppet with loosened strings, grasping at the window glass with sweat-slick fingers that don't have a chance in hell of finding traction. He falls with me, to his knees, somehow still inside me. Still moving. Weakly, I fall forward, presenting my ass to him as the world looms below, watching as he claims me. The sky observes unfeelingly as the water churns, laughing at my destruction.

Far too soon, I hear him groan and I'm flooded with fire.

"Like this," he bites out, collapsing against my back. "Only feel like this."

* * *

THE INTENSITY of the moment flickers and dies like a candle being blown out. Minutes later, we disentangle our limbs, scrambling to find a safe distance apart. I crawl to the farthest corner of the room while he approaches the desk. Then I notice an incessant buzzing sound: a phone ringing.

"What is it?" he snaps, his back to me. Suddenly, his shoulders slump and he braces his free hand against the desk. "What? She's awake? Keep her in bed until I get there."

A sudden urgency stiffens his spine. He grabs his pants from the floor, wrenching them up. Only one person could spur him into action like this.

"Is she all right?" Without sex or rage to distract, the full depth of my selfishness sinks in. Poor Masha. Her brother should have been by her side last night. Not chasing after me. Though something tells me that the other day's events were not an out-of-the-blue occurrence.

"She's fine." He sounds as though he had to spit out every word, aware of the promise he made. *Talk to me.* After doing up his zipper, he rakes his fingers through his hair and curses. His clothes are crumpled, damp with sweat. Sighing, he peels them off while stumbling for the door.

"I'm coming with you." I don't know where the desire comes from. Maybe it's pathetic self-preservation. I can't face myself alone. I can't face the marks, and the aftermath, without him to consume my attention. Not yet.

He looks back sharply, still tugging his pants off. I picture him heading for the shower. He'll barge into Bolles wearing a day-old suit and a crazed expression, but he can't reveal that part of himself to her. He'll clean and scrape the broken pieces of himself together. He'll put his mask on. Pretend.

In the end, he says nothing, but I sense rather than feel the unspoken command. *Hurry up.*

I lurch to my feet, using the window for balance. Then I follow him up the stairs. He enters the room I woke up in, while I creep into the navy one. I snatch items of clothing at random from the closet and shower, scrubbing at my skin without surveying the damage. Sore. Burning. Bleeding.

I dry quickly and reenter the hall minutes later wearing a black dress and a pair of flats. I find him waiting for me at the base of the steps, his damp hair dripping onto the shoulders of a black suit. Watching me, he adjusts a gray tie, looking no less exhausted than he did before.

"Are you ready?"

I swallow at the grating tone in his voice. "Yes."

Together, we take the elevator down to the lower level. A car is already waiting in the garage, a stern-faced driver at the helm. We have no choice but to share the back seat. Gritting his teeth, Blake holds the door open for me. I swear I hear him inhale as I settle onto the seat. Then he climbs in beside me, slamming the door behind us.

Minutes tick by in silence as the driver maneuvers the car onto the main street. Glaring daylight leaves nothing to hide behind. I still feel him in my skin. Taste him on my lips. Our damp hair drips steadily, creating a pulsing soundtrack. Too loud.

"Masha," I say, breaking the silence. "Is she...all right?" I'm not talking physically.

"I..." He breaks off and swallows. Lightning quick, his hand shoots out, grasping mine.

My eyes widen at the contact. There's no rage in his grip. If anything, his fingers shake, demanding whatever strength I have left to give.

"Her father never saw her for the first five years of her life. Her mother and he divorced. She took Masha away. Kept her isolated. Then she remarried. A monster."

Oh no. A part of me suspects the direction this tale will take. In a sad, ironic way, Masha has the look for it: the tragic princess in a brutal fairytale.

"What happened?" I force myself to ask when he doesn't continue.

I gasp. His grip tightens as he glares out of his window. "The bastard controlled her. Manipulated her. Warped her mind. When she was barely seventeen, he forced her to marry a man just as twisted as he was."

"Oh God." Like a punch to the chest—that's how perspective shifts around me.

Forrest Hollings was no saint, but even he had lines he never crossed. Perhaps he thought he could save me for the highest bidder. Luckily, he died before ever getting the chance.

"Her husband was…cruel," Blake says simply. "It was fucking hell to get her away from him. Her father—*our* father—made me promise to keep her from the motherfucker. And I did. I paid him off. Threatened him. Blackmailed. Nothing ever worked for long. Six months ago, he managed to contact her again, and he hasn't stopped since. I offered him more money. Hired thugs to teach him a lesson. In the end, I brought her here, to the States. A week ago, he found her again."

Raw pain enhances his features, exaggerating the small nuances I missed before. The black stubble growing in along his chin. The overgrown length to his hair. The bruises beneath his eyes, far darker than they first seemed. How long has it been since he's slept?

Maybe not since that night in Hollings Manor.

"She'll be fine in a few days," he adds, though I think he's speaking more to himself than to me. "And if he comes near her again, I'll fucking kill him."

"Have you gone to the police?" I ask, marveling at the fact that he still has my hand. Tension radiates through his skin, as if he's deliberately avoiding squeezing too hard. Crushing me.

"The police don't mean shit to a man with money." He lets me go, and my hand cools without his heat. "If I pay him off, he'll just come back again."

We say nothing else during the rest of the trip to the hospital. Rather than a normal room on a medical floor, Masha has a private suite in a locked unit. A realm I know all too well. Some of the nurses call me by name as we enter, a fact that doesn't go unnoticed.

"How many times?" Blake asks as we cross the quiet unit with its soothing, light-blue walls and gentle atmosphere. His expression is strained as we pass a patient, thin as a rail, trailing an IV pole as she wanders the wing.

How many times have I been in Masha's place? "Too many times," I reply.

His sister is in bed when we finally reach her room. Pale sunlight streams in through a large window, illuminating a vase of yellow roses on her bedside table.

"Son of a bitch." Blake crosses the room and snatches the blossoms from the table, tossing them into the trash. Then he sinks to his knees beside Masha's bed and smooths his hand over her hair, coaxing her awake. A worn smile makes him look like a different man—someone capable of joy.

They converse in German, their voices hushed, and I step into the hall rather than intrude.

Not long after, he returns to my side. "I... She's asking to speak to you."

"Really?" I look over, surprised to find slightly less exhaustion weighing his features down than before.

"If you don't want to, I could—"

"No." I shake my head. "No, I'll see her."

I slip past him and warily enter the hospital room. Masha is upright, propped against a wall of pillows. She looks pale in the faint light drifting in through one of the wide windows, but a fragile smile shapes her mouth.

"Hello," she says, her voice faint and lilting.

I do my best to match her grin, praying that none of my concern shows. She's just a waif beneath white sheets, almost the same color as the linens. Her hair forms a golden halo, which adds some definition to her pale form. Dark circles enhance her hollow gaze, making it seem endless. Penetrating.

"How are you feeling?" I ask, approaching the side of her bed.

She laughs weakly. "You don't have to pretend," she says. "I know that I scared you. I know how I look. At least someone can see the obvious." Her gaze cuts beyond me to the doorway, and a hint of what could be pain distorts the green irises. "I read the papers," she croaks, clutching the blankets draped around her. "He promised me he wouldn't… Be honest with me—"

"They were lies." Driven by an impulse I can't name, I reach for one of her hands and clench it tight. "He never assaulted me."

"But he did hurt you," Masha says firmly. "I know he did."

My lips twitch to form a rebuttal. Maybe not for Blake's sake, but for his sister's peace of mind. As exhausted and frail as she looks, there's a coldness I vaguely recognize in her gaze: resigned fear. She doesn't want to see him as a monster. At the same time, she's not naïve.

"I... He didn't hurt me," I say, but the words fall flat. Hollow.

Masha sighs and stares down at her hands. "You don't have to lie to me." Gingerly, she disentangles her fingers from mine and turns to stare out the nearest window. "Sometimes... I'm so sick of being the victim. The pawn. Even Blake. I love him so much, but he's the same." Her gaze meets mine, burning brightly for the first time during this visit. "Maybe the only way to beat them is at their own game."

I say nothing. Her words resonate deeply enough without requiring agreement out loud. Their game: vicious lies and cruel manipulation. Could I ever be so callous?

"Thank you for coming," Masha says, snapping me from my thoughts.

I awkwardly back away and reenter the hallway, where I find Blake lingering near the doorway, his expression tense.

One glance at me and he grits his teeth, nodding just once. "Let's go."

We return to the car, but I don't recognize the direction the driver heads in.

"Lunch," Blake proposes, sounding hesitant. "Or a walk. Or a fucking drive around the city. Anything to…to just talk."

Hope flares to life in my chest, a painful, pathetic thing. "Okay. A drive."

The driver may be listening, but this moment feels too damn fragile.

"What did Masha say to you?"

I don't miss the careful note in his voice. "Nothing," I say, but the truth is obvious in what I don't voice. She asked me if he was a monster, and I couldn't find the words to deny it. "She looks better, at least," I finish, stumbling over the words. "Healthy—"

"She'll be fine," he says. "I've arranged to have her transferred to a more familiar facility upstate. She'll…she'll be fine."

Again, he alludes to the fact that this isn't her first stint in a hospital. A part of me wants to demand more answers, but I keep seeing her face, that fragile innocence. In the end, all I can do is stare out the window and picture how I must have appeared to my brothers when I was in her place. Maybe I was too selfish to see it before, but now, their concern makes a bit more sense and I hate myself for causing it.

"It feels strange to be back," Blake says, breaking the silence. "I…I thought about you." He takes my hand, this time cradling my fingers against his palm. "Every damn day. God, I thought of you…"

Words fight to squeeze their way past my thickening throat only to fail. I thought of him too. Every moment. Every second. I couldn't not think of him.

"Those days," he adds, his voice deepening, "I play them over and over. They feel like a fucking dream. Sometimes… I wonder if it was even real. If any of it was real."

"It was." It had to be, because those days were all I had left. I still cling to them like an addict to her very last vial of poison.

"I still remember." He laughs, the sound broken, echoing off the close quarters. "Your laugh. Those stories we used to tell."

"Humpty Dumpty," I say, my voice barely a whisper.

"Yes." He nods. His other hand captures my chin, tilting my face toward his. He's closer, his mouth nudging mine, a silent demand to open. He doesn't kiss me when I do. He merely breathes, inhaling every breath I exhale. "I know that things can't ever be like they were. But…I want. I need…"

"I know."

We say nothing else, spending what feels like an eternity trapped in an intimate embrace, sharing the same air. The same space. The same pain.

We can't ever go back. Brandt Lloyd is dead, along with his fiery princess, Snow.

We're the jagged shells of those two innocent souls, left behind, forced to find some semblance of self again.

But maybe we can find a way to meld our broken edges.

Or stab each other with them.

THIRTEEN

BLAKE

SHE ALWAYS WAS the only person in the world who could make the ugliest situations reveal their beauty. Like finding solace in a mental institution or crafting an imaginary world for a boy desperate to escape his own personal hell.

They used to wonder why I spent so much time with her —*them*, the onlookers and gossips and petty, spiteful neighbors. Maybe I was deranged? Or degenerate? Or awkward with people my own age?

But they were wrong.

The silly little girl with stars in her eyes could make an afternoon shut indoors with only books to read compelling. To her, nothing was ordinary. A bad day was the worst one in the universe—for that moment. A good one, the very best, at least until the next.

She always saw magic in every moment.

And she always ignored the darkness in me.

"You're thinking." Her fingers dance a trail up my forearm, luring me back to the present. Halfway up my elbow she pauses, her gaze lowered as if registering the act for the first time. Silently, she pulls away.

But I stop her.

"About us," I say, maneuvering her wrist so that her palm is upright. "You really were a pain in the ass."

She gasps, playfully offended. "I was *your* pain in the ass." Her face falls as the full weight of her words lands between us.

My pain in the ass. Just not anymore.

Something in my expression must change because she sighs and tries pulling her hand away. "I'm sorry—"

"You don't have to walk on eggshells around me." I let her go and turn my attention to the nearest window. The world passes by in a blur, and I indulge the dramatic irony: ten years without her have passed much in the same way.

A blur. Colorless and empty.

"I feel like…" She sighs, fidgeting beside me. Her hands run aimlessly through her hair, twisting the soft curls. "I feel like I've forgotten how to say the right thing. It didn't use to be this hard."

Hard. My jaw clenches at her use of the word and I can't fucking help myself. "Was it easier with him? Daniel Ellingston?"

She inhales sharply. "Please don't do this."

"I don't mean it like that." Fuck, maybe she's right. It's so fucking hard. "I mean in that… He didn't scare you. I do."

She can't deny it. Even now she sits angled toward the door on her end, maintaining a hairsbreadth of distance between us at all times. Her eyes dart warily toward mine and then away again.

"You don't scare me." I have to strain to hear her. "You don't. I scare myself. Because every time you lash out. Every time you flinch when you look at me, I remember…"

She doesn't have to say it.

I remember who you used to be.

A person I can never be again.

"Do you want me to leave?" I keep my tone intentionally soft as my entire body stiffens. I feel like a fucking fool at the gallows, waiting to be hung on her say so.

"No," she says and some of the tension in my body eases. "But… Can I ask you something?"

"Yes." She jumps and as my voice echoes back to me, I realize how goddamn eager I sounded. Feral. "I mean, you can ask me anything."

"Masha's...fine," she says, testing out my term. "But what about you?"

I clench my jaw, steeling myself for what she might say. "What do you mean?"

She swallows hard and then tentatively adds, "Do you still have those nightmares?"

My blood runs cold. Nightmares. That's a delicate word for it—when she really means waking up, shouting like a fucking madman, chasing phantoms in the dark.

"I shouldn't have asked," she says quickly. "It's none of my business—"

"I don't like talking about it," I admit, hating how cold I sound.

She nods, her hands fluttering over her lap. "My brothers had me hospitalized after the gala. Did you know that?"

Her words land like a sucker punch—not that she intends for them to. Redness paints her cheeks. Embarrassment? Before I can be sure, she turns away from me again, eyeing the view passing beyond the windows. "Their one condition was that I see my therapist once a week—and I haven't even called to set up one appointment. Why?" She shakes her head and fingers one of her loose curls. My own hand twitches, aching to tuck the strand behind her ear. Like I used to I realize.

She'd play with her hair whenever that bastard Forrest said something that sent her running to one of her hiding places. I'd chase her down and smooth my fingers through the tangled mess she made. Always.

"Why?" I prod as her silence extends to nearly a minute. "Why not?"

She inhales, her face tilted toward me a fraction of an inch. "Because despite what happened recently... We both know where the true damage is."

An answer springs to my lips. "The past."

She nods. "And I don't think I'm brave enough to go there. Not yet. I can't—"

"I know." I don't smother the impulse to touch her this time. She stiffens when I ease the mangled curl from her grasp. It's still soft, despite the damage done by a forced hair-cut and cheap dye. The damage *I* did.

"Have you gone to therapy?" I can hear the skepticism in her voice.

"No," I admit, frowning. "What could I say?"

That I was convicted of a crime that I didn't commit, accused by the girl I loved. That the man I believed was my father liked screwing the neighbor's wife—when he wasn't smacking me across the face for fucking breathing.

Anger seeps in and for a cruel second, I'm back there. In that place. As *that* kid. I'd take every blow without a word. Or complaint. I never fought back.

Until now, I never understood why.

"Blake?" Snow runs her fingers down the side of my jaw, and I know she's reliving it too. The many times she would trace my bruises while simultaneously pretending they didn't exist. "Are you alright?"

I shrug her off, swallowing hard, squashing those memories. "I'm fine."

But I'm not. My gaze hones in on her fingers, so soft and slim. In them—figuratively—she has a whole wealth of information to use against me, if she wanted to. My past. Her pain. The worst part? I couldn't stop her if she decided to.

If. And if she did, my first instinct is one I never felt when Harrison Lloyd raised his fist. With him, I cowered. But against her?

I *want* to fight. Bite. Snarl.

That bastard could beat the shit out of me, but I never felt wounded. Harrison Lloyd could never truly hurt me.

Snow on the other hand? She could leave me. Turn against me. Hate me...

And there's no need for a goddamn therapist to spell out what would happen next.

Her betrayal cuts deeper than any bruise.

And if I'm at her mercy again...

She'd fucking decimate me.

* * *

SNOWY

WE RETURN TO THE SUITE, retreating to separate rooms as if by an unspoken agreement. The need to lick my wounds drives me into the bathroom and I strip, climbing into the tub and turning the water to the hottest setting. Steaming.

Outstretched beneath the scalding liquid, I feel no closer to sanity than I did the first night I dared to take on Blake Lorenz. God, I was so stupid back then, barely three months ago. I was a fool.

And now?

I'm reckless. My mind goes to Masha and the torment that drove her to the unthinkable. But was I ever any different? I let my emotions shape my weight, knowing what I was doing to everyone around me. I knew the risks.

But when I wanted to fall...I stubbornly fell.

Only one boy was ever there to catch me. To shake his head at my broken pieces and instruct that I put them back together myself. King's men or king's horses couldn't mend me; only I could do that. Only he would force me to.

But, now, that boy's grown up, and the king's lost his softer edge. He'll break me apart sooner than he'll put me back together. It's the only way we know how to coexist.

The sound of a door opening snaps me into awareness. I jump, realizing I never locked the door to the bedroom or the bathroom. Both are easily flung aside, revealing a creature with eyes blazing like hellfire.

"B-Blake?" I scramble to cover myself, not that his eyes ever leave my face. It's as if he fixes his gaze on mine deliberately, honed with rage. "What's wrong?"

"Interesting conversation you and Sloane had," he snarls, throwing something at me.

It lands in the bathwater with a splash and I scramble to catch it before it can sink. The unfortunate object turns out to be a tabloid, its cover soaked through.

"You want me to be honest, but have you been?" he demands while I read the scandalous headline: **ABUSED HEIRESS TELLS ALL.**

My heart sinks as I scan the first few sentences. *With allegations of abuse against Blake Lorenz from heiress Snowy Hollings swirling, a close personal friend of the heiress tells us she regrets her failed engagement to Daniel Ellingston...*

Oh, Sloane. I don't even blame her. Our relationship was always transactional.

"You can't even fucking deny it. I knew it. I fucking knew better than to let down my guard around the *irresistible* Snow." Blake barks out a hollow laugh, shaking his head. There's almost a desperation to the action—relief? "And there it is," he adds nastily, "that goddamn thing only you can make me feel." He forms a fist, bringing it toward his heart as if he means to pummel it from his chest. At the last minute, he storms from the room.

Exhausted, I sink back, tossing the magazine aside. My eyes drift shut, and I focus intently on the warmth seeping into my aching muscles, buying myself more time before I have to face reality beyond these walls. So many false stops and starts. This one feels like yet another vicious yank backward. At the same time, I suspect that the rumor was nothing more than an excuse. The first thing he could latch onto to guard himself again.

Because this scares him.

It's terrifying me.

Eventually the water cools too much. I can't hide here anymore, and I crawl into a towel without bothering to dry myself first. Dripping wet, I enter the hall, wandering with grim determination into that darkened room at the very end.

He's sitting on the bed, his back to me. Faint moonlight sneaking through the curtains gives his hulking shape vague definition, dusting his hair and outlining his shoulders. They're hunched, radiating tension as I cross the threshold.

"Get out."

I don't. Instead, I let my steps carry me carefully over the bare floors, swaying to keep my balance. Both of my hands clutch the towel to my front, and in the end, I let it fall before mounting the mattress. "You don't get to storm away every time something pisses you off," I admonish, my tone deliberately soft. "You promised we could talk. So talk—"

"Stop it." He lurches to his feet and marches toward the windows, stubbornly eyeing the sliver of view visible. "Not now, Snow."

"Come here and *talk* to me." My voice rings out, stronger than it should be considering that I'm breathless, gasping for air.

He growls, almost snarling in frustration. "I said get the fuck out—"

"Then come to bed at least." I flatten my hand against the space beside me, loud enough for him to hear. "Come lay beside me. You look exhausted."

"No." His teeth are bared, visible in his snarling profile. But it's more of a plea than a refusal. Wavering control humanizes him like nothing else. I can see it fighting to combat the hate he seems desperate to cling to.

"Blake," I say, calling him by name. "Come lay beside me."

"I'm not a goddamn child." He turns, his body hunched forward, his eyes narrowed. "And I told you to get the fuck out—"

For the first time, he seems to realize just how I must appear: wet and naked, outstretched on his bed. Submitting. He swallows hard, his expression wavering.

As the cold air assaults my damp skin, I extend my hand. "Come."

A curse escapes through his clenched teeth, but the next second, he advances like a man possessed. The bed lurches beneath his weight as he lies down with his back to me. Carefully, I shift toward him, letting my fingers sink through his hair before he can rake his own through the wild curls. A sigh runs through him, jolting me in the aftermath. He doesn't relax into me. Never lets down his guard.

All he does is close his eyes with a begrudging hiss.

And I give him five minutes of silence. Of peace.

But then I can't resist.

"Do you remember?" I ask in a whisper, still stroking his hair as much as I dare. My fingers twitch sporadically, gliding through the wild strands, but he doesn't call me off. Yet. "You never could sleep when something was on your mind."

He tenses at the mention of the past, his unease acting like a shield, threatening to cut him off already. "I remember a lot of things about the past," he says, his tone laced with warning.

This time, I don't back down from the threat. "So do I."

He sighs but doesn't offer up a cutting retort. Progress? Or maybe an ominous sign.

"I remember that you used to pester me when I couldn't," he admits. "You'd never… You never let anything go."

I nod. "Not until you told me what was wrong."

The answer would always be a multitude of different thoughts or concerns most boys his age wouldn't bother to care about. His future. His family. The perils of the universe.

Something warns me that none of those topics are what's bothering him now. Not even close.

"You always told me in the end," I hear myself say almost wistfully. "Always…"

He doesn't respond this time—but it isn't until I hear the slow cadence of his breathing that I realize why.

He fell asleep.

* * *

I WAKE UP ALONE, unsurprisingly. He had another nightmare last night, shouting at phantoms in the dark. I closed my eyes and pretended to be asleep, though I doubt I fooled him. Despair and dread wafted from his skin like perfume, leaving a trail I can still follow as pale daylight illuminates the otherwise monochrome room.

He's waiting for me in the study, hunched over a breakfast tray piled high with too many foods to name. Bacon. Eggs. Bagels. I can't help imagining a fallen warrior presenting his opponent with a lavish feast as a form of surrender. Or a challenge.

He nods to the chair strategically placed before the spread, and a dare lurks beneath his gaze as he lifts a fork and extends it to me. "Eat."

Smart soldiers choose their battles wisely. With Hunter, I knew his deliveries of meals came only out of love and concern. Blake, however, merely wants to provoke. He needs me to refuse him now; it's the only way he knows how to turn the tables in retaliation for what little vulnerability I coaxed from him last night.

Today, I'm too damn tired to play the game. I sit as commanded and dutifully shovel a spoonful of yogurt into my mouth. He watches, scowling at the subtle defiance. Regardless, with every subsequent bite, his frown lessens. Soon, he's merely resigned as I polish off the serving of eggs.

"Your spoils, princess," he says mockingly while sliding a strip of paper in my direction. A check. One for a disgusting sum. "It's merely for show," he admits. "Our accountants will need to do the necessary paperwork for the transfer."

"I don't want it."

He looks like I've slapped him, and I race to clarify.

"I'd prefer you donated it. To Haven. In honor of women like Masha."

The mention of his sister only earns me a shred of leniency. "So content you are with Harrison Lloyd's money that you can't accept a dime of mine. Is that it, Snow?"

"No!" I push back from the table, gritting my teeth.

Only he can do this to me. Maybe he was right; we can only feel anything when together. Hate. And Lust. And *pain*—all at once. It's an unhealthy mixture, and every time we clash, I feel in danger of overdosing.

"I don't need your money. I don't need anyone's money."

"Don't lie to me," he warns, a cold smile shaping his mouth. "What about Daniel Ellingston's money? When he had some, anyway? You were more than willing to sell yourself to him for it."

It's a low blow, and it takes everything I have in me not to jump at the bait. Something must have happened in between his nightmare and when I woke up. Before that, even. A catalyst for him trying to pick a fight over the tabloid, perhaps. Something has him jumpy, itching for a battle, and my stomach sinks at the thought of what it might be.

"Don't forget that I sold myself to you, too," I say softly.

He frowns and retreats to the windows. The breathtaking view only seems to earn his ire. He scowls at the skyline. "Keep some of the money—"

"Half, then," I concede. "Donate half of it to Haven."

"Fine." He snatches up the check and stows it into his pocket. Then he sighs, and I see a hint of what has him so irritable. Unease. "I...I need..."

"Anything." Damn. I didn't mean to sound so eager. So fucking desperate. But I am. Extortion and blackmail—the only dynamic in which we seem to function. And I'll take it over the fighting or the insults. "I mean... Just tell me what you want me to do."

"Accompany me to a ball. Tomorrow night."

I blink. "A ball?"

"Rumors are rampant, Snow," he says, sounding almost neutral for once. He sinks onto the chair across from me and absently snatches up my hand. His fingers stroke the back of it, grinding warmth into my skin. "They're a bigger threat than expected. They're pressuring me to step down from the board. And I'll admit that I wanted to rip down everything with the Hollings name—but I spent almost half my life being groomed to run that company."

He still wants it. I can see the desire burning in his eyes. The same one that drives Hunter to lie and scheme his way toward the top of the corporate ladder. Power.

"So you need me there."

"No." He hesitates, trying to find the right words. "I *want* you there."

"I pick my dress?"

He shoots me an odd look. "Yes…"

"And no lying. No blackmail. No hidden extortion?" I almost expect him to say yes.

Instead, he shakes his head. "I'm asking you for a favor, Snow," he admits.

One with supposedly no strings attached.

"All right. I'll do it."

"Good." He releases me and rises to his feet. The sudden shift to his expression takes my breath away. It's so easy for him to switch emotion on and off.

A pang runs through my chest, a painful tendril of doubt. "But I want something in return."

"Oh?" He cocks his head. From his posture alone, I can guess what he suspects I'll demand: something humiliating or degrading. Something to shift the scales in my favor.

"I want you…" I inhale raggedly, meeting his gaze, hiding nothing. "I want *you* for a day. You. No lies. No games. No secrets. I want to talk to *you*."

No. I didn't mean to say that. But any excuse I may have dies in the face of his expression. He's guarded again, so damn wary. Like a predator eyeing a trap, he looks me over from head to toe.

"A day?"

"Are you afraid?" I wonder, letting my voice dip to a mocking octave. Perhaps joking can lessen the fear building in my veins, warning that I've gone too far, too fast. "The big, bad Blake Lorenz afraid of one little bargain?"

"A day," he repeats skeptically. "I thought I just paid for the privilege."

I flinch. "Don't mock me."

"I'm not." He runs a hand through his hair, knocking the wildest curls away from his face. "Fine. A day. To do what?"

I stare at my half-eaten plate, suddenly overwhelmed. From the corner of my eye, I notice the bookshelf. It's almost like I knew all along what I'd find there, taken from my purse, shoved to the very end of the selection of books. I stand, aware of him watching, and grab the leather volume before offering it to him.

"I want you to read to me."

"Snow…"

"Please."

He eyes the book like it's something dangerous. A venomous threat waiting to strike. He takes it anyway, crossing over to the threshold of the room, and I follow him without being beckoned, trailing his slow footsteps into the living room, over to the red throne-like chair.

He sits, cocking his head to issue another silent dare. This one I don't shy away from. I sink onto his lap, facing the view. Gradually, my body relaxes into his firmer one. His arms come around my waist as he opens the book. Then, grudgingly, he starts to read.

His voice sinks to a low, grating rasp that transports me to another time. Another place, with another man. But, for the first time, those two halves don't battle for supremacy. They merely coexist: memory and reality.

"And all the king's horses and all the king's men failed to put him back together again."

I shiver as he bats a strip of hair from my neck. And then he reads again.

And again.

And again, retelling the same tale until the daylight fades around us.

FOURTEEN

I STARTLE TO AWARENESS, curled in an awkward position against a firmer surface. Warm fingers part my hair into sections, and a part of me shivers in recognition. I know this feeling. This smell. More and more, my nostalgia acts like poison, and with every breath, I'm overwhelmed by memory.

We used to lie like this sometimes, huddled together like magnets. Though perhaps old Snowy would describe it more poetically: We used to exist together, like two halves of the same broken, abominable creature.

"You're so damn beautiful," he murmurs when I start to stir.

My heart pangs, uneasy. Only God knows how long he let me sleep like this, bundled in his arms. The city glows below us, a hotbed of neon fire and ebony darkness. Damn. I rub my eyes, mourning the loss of time.

"How late is it?" I whisper.

He shrugs, his eyes unreadable in the dim illumination. "Close to midnight."

"But still today." Heart in my throat, I turn, craning my neck so that I can see his face as I reach for the collar of the shirt. "You're still mine. I mean…under our agreement."

His jaw twitches as if to issue a refusal, but in the end, he lets me slowly unhook every button and drag the sleeves down one by one, leaving his chest bare. Why?

Maybe I'm finally letting myself believe what he said: that we can only ever understand each other like this. With physical touch over words. In silence and darkness, and devoid of trust.

His past will always be a barrier to overcome. If he won't tell me in words, then I'll have to feel the damage for myself.

And there's so much of it to discover.

My pulse surges as I stand, circle around to his back, and allow my fingers to knead his shoulders, sensing the tension coiled there. But my finger slips, finding a nasty patch of circular flesh, eerily smooth. "How?" I ask, though I already know the answer.

"Spoiled, rich bastards weren't very popular in prison," he says, his voice rough. "Especially perverted ones."

I swallow hard, tears burning behind my eyes, and withdraw my hands. "I'm sorry—"

"Don't." He grabs my wrist, forcing the contact.

Fighting apprehension back, I spread my fingers out again, flattening my palms along his spine. "C-can you tell me what happened—"

"*No.*" He shakes his head, softening his tone. "I-I mean…I can't go there, Snow. Not like this."

Fair enough. Slowly, I trace a ragged scar, cringing at the images my own imagination conjures: him pinned down, tortured. Because of me.

"How many are there?"

He hesitates. I can feel the vibrations of his lungs as they struggle to trap the answer inside.

"Twenty…thirty," he says finally. "I don't really know."

"Turn around."

He lets me guide him so that he's sitting with his back exposed, still facing the windows. A low sound catches in the air as I sink to my knees. It's like he can sense what I offer without having to see it: submission. I press the silent promise into his skin, brushing my lips along the ridge of his hip. Two scars etched onto him by my foolish mistake.

"Three," I murmur, lathing my tongue over another healed scar. "Four. Five."

He sucks in a breath with every exploration, and I can almost taste the need in his skin, which feeds the ache building inside me. It comes from nowhere, hot like fire— and he stokes it higher with every bit his grip on the edge of the chair tightens, straining the muscles in his back.

He says nothing when I stand and circle to his front. Then I kneel again, meeting his gaze. All I find is…reverence, for once, and it chokes me. Neon colors paint his skin as I shuffle between his legs and work on the front of his pants.

"Goddamn…" He inhales sharply and groans through an exhalation. His large hands cup my scalp, trembling even before I find his cock, which is hardening beneath my touch, and coax him from the cage of fabric. "Jesus, Snow."

I part my lips, and he bucks his hips, gripping my hair tightly in his fist. I'm stuffed to the brim with him. I'm choking on him, and it's a devastating death. I let him use me as he needs to, writhing his way to a slow-building orgasm that catches me off guard. He grunts, flooding my mouth, and instinct nearly overrides the need to please him. My throat contracts, but at the last second, I force myself to swallow.

Every drop.

"Shit!" He shoves me back and I release him with a wet pop, gasping for air. "So good." He smooths his fingers along my face, murmuring praises. "So fucking good."

I rest my cheek against his thigh as his fingers sink through my hair and pet the thick curls. And I don't know how long we remain like that.

I just wish it could fucking last.

FIFTEEN

BLAKE

HOLDING HER IN MY ARMS, I'm at the mercy of the cruelest weapon that Snowy Hollings has in her arsenal.

Peace. Nothing compares to this. Not the money I stand to gain from the destruction of her family's company. Not the years of torment she caused. Not even the true extent of the twisted web I've spun around her.

For a few minutes of golden dawn, she's perfect, her chest rising softly, her hair falling across her face—and the rest of the world fades away. I can pretend like this, for a second, that I've finally won her back.

Screw Lyle Harlow or Daniel Ellingston.

Screw the world waiting beyond these walls. Hearing her breathe, sensing the warmth from her skin, inhaling her scent shouldn't be more than enough to smother the rest.

But it is.

And...for fuck's sake, I want to hate her for it.

My fingers twitch, smoothing the shorn curls from her face. Her delicate bone structure plays with the faint rays of the rising sun, reflecting it off pure white skin. It paints her in a golden hue—a mocking reminder of what she is in the grand scheme.

A trophy I desired to win at all fucking costs.

But she's so much more.

We could have *been* so much more.

Groaning with regret, I stand and carry her in my arms to a leather chaise. She stirs lightly as I set her down on it and back away. Upstairs her scent chases me, even into the shower.

I do my best to scrub her away, pretending that it would be so easy. Snow clings to my skin, but a few lathers of soap can wash her off. It's futile of course—the woman is in my blood.

She's always been there.

Always.

And the moment she sees the monster I really am, she'll run away again.

This time for good.

Across the room, my phone vibrates on a dresser. It's as if the universe itself decided to issue a fucking challenge. *You think you can keep her?*

Think again.

"Blake." I snarl, answering the phone without looking at the ID. For a damn good reason.

No one sane would call this early.

"I warned you, you sick bastard," a man slurs into my ear. "I warned you to stay away from her. Don't hang up," he warns before I even start to lower the phone, intending to do just that. "You listen to me. You think I'll let you hurt her again? Hell no."

"And just how do you plan on doing that?" Somehow my tone comes out level. Some fucking how. Maybe it's instinct, warning me that this time, he isn't bluffing.

"I'll tell you how," he says. "I'll tell her the truth. That's what I'll do. I'll tell her everything. Everything you've done. I'll tell her…that it was you from the start."

* * *

SNOWY

HOT SUNLIGHT WARMS my naked skin. He must have placed me on the chaise in the living room without bothering to cover me.

Because rather than sleep, he spent the night watching over me. Sure enough, I sense his gaze as I draw my legs together and peel my eyes open to a high ceiling.

"Your breakfast is on the table." His voice comes from the upstairs landing, and like any addict, I chase it. He's there at the top of the steps, adjusting a pair of silver cufflinks, dressed to the nines in tailored business attire: a gray suit, a white shirt, and a navy tie. "Eat," he warns when he sees me mount the topmost step. Something unreadable crosses his expression. Uncertainty? Before I can place it for sure, he leans forward, swiping his lips along my forehead, and I'm rendered speechless. "Eat," he insists as I marvel over what's as close to an affectionate gesture as a man like him can give. "I need to go to the office, but I'll return later."

I watch him draw back, a frown tugging at my mouth. How soon the real world chooses to descend. It's as if there's this vicious tug of war between the moments when we come close to a semblance of intimacy and those when he feels farther away than ever before.

Resigned, I grab a robe from my room and find food waiting for me in the study. Blake hasn't left yet, and a thought begins to itch at the back of my skull, impossible to soothe. Ronan and Hunter. Placated or not, they'll happily ambush Blake Lorenz in public if they believe for a second he's hurt me in any way. Sighing, I reach for the office phone and dial the hotel directly, intending to leave a message.

Instead, Ronan answers, his voice gruff. "Who is this?"

"It's me," I stammer.

"Snowy, thank God. Where are you?" He sounds strained, as if it's taking all of his effort to keep from shouting. "I'll come. Just tell me where."

"I'm safe," I say, avoiding the question. "I promise. But…" I glance at the clock. Blake is already late, but Ronan? Never. "Why aren't you at the office?"

"Snowy, what are you talking about?"

"I… Didn't you get a seat on the board?"

He laughs coldly. "You mean that shitty olive branch Lorenz offered? One seat for Hunter and me to fight over between the two of us? I let Hunter take it."

One seat?

The receiver slips from my grip, landing on the desk. I can hear Ronan calling for me, but nothing registers over the rage surging through my veins, deafening me. I'm racing into the foyer before I know it, catching him heading toward the elevator.

"I'll have a car sent around seven to bring you to the…" He stiffens at my expression. When I form a fist and smash it against his chest, he doesn't even flinch.

"One seat?" I shout. "One goddamn seat?"

"It's all I could risk," he says, not even trying to hide it. "With my position already in peril, I would have been laughed out of the building if I'd proposed to restore two

Hollingses now. I made a calculated move by installing Hunter first. I always intended to add Ronan when I could afford to spend the capital."

"A move," I echo. "Perhaps a better word is a *game*. Another way for you to watch my brothers fight over their goddamn birthright."

Danger flashes in his eyes. "And what about my birthright, Snow?"

"I don't know," I admit, stepping back. "I don't even know who you are anymore. You aren't Brandt Lloyd."

Anger. It hardens him like nothing else, twisting his features into a chilling mask. "And who do we have to thank for that?"

I shake my head, blinking rapidly. "I won't let you make me spend the rest of my life apologizing. Not after everything you've done to me!"

"Then don't," he says, his teeth gritted. "And I won't dare expect you to give me anything else. Feel free to leave, Snow."

Exasperation forms a pathetic response. "I don't want to fight. I just... I just want you to stop pushing me away."

He turns, heading for the door. "Stop letting me." Then the elevator doors open and close with him behind them and he's gone.

* * *

I DON'T STORM from the penthouse, crying tears of despair. I pace instead, tearing at my hair as I run over every word. Every phrase. Every kiss and fuck and touch. My parting words ring truer than ever: *Stop pushing me away.*

And his are equally enlightening.

Stop letting me.

God, everything about him feels like a test. A game. How far can he push me before I run? Before I break? How far can Snowy bend before she lets him down again?

A part of me rails at the treatment. How dare he dangle trust like a carrot he'll never let me have? But there's the true heart of the matter: I did have it once. By all intents and purposes, I threw it away.

But that doesn't mean I deserve this. Or do I?

Doubt haunts me every fucking minute I stay within these walls. Rather than leave, I'm driven farther into the maze of rooms, eventually finding my way inside the navy one. Without thinking, I finger an emerald gown and then rip it from the hanger. Another. A whole damn rack of clothing tossed onto the floor. I once thought these pieces of silk and satin made me who I was—Snowy Hollings. But who am I really?

A rumpled pile of couture gowns can't tell me.

Panting, I work my way through the entire closet, grasping, tearing, throwing. Fittingly, the last dress I reach for holds the most significance.

I have no idea how he found it—or if he even looked inside the black garment bag. I hid it at the very back of my old wardrobe, if only to stop myself from trying it on every five damn minutes.

My fingers shake as I undo the zipper now, freeing the dress for the first time in months. As always, an appreciative gasp catches in my throat. This floor-length creation of white silk was my dream wedding dress. Ironically, I chose it without my fiancé in mind. It was the gown of a fairytale princess, with lace sleeves, a sloping neckline, and a body-hugging bodice. In lieu of a veil, I intended to wear flowers in my hair, otherwise adorned only by my wedding ring.

But that was then. Now, it's just another worthless item, but I stop shy of tossing it aside. Instead, I carry it into the bathroom like a spoil of war.

If Blake Lorenz wants to play a game of guilt and blame, then I'll take the next round.

Carefully, I drape my gown over the counter. Then I face my reflection, eyeing the woman staring back. Her eyes are reddened, but she hasn't cried yet. Gritting my teeth, I ensure that she won't.

Then I turn to the shower and run the water as hot as I can stand it.

Hot like hellfire.

SIXTEEN

THE FACT that I find a car waiting for me at seven feels more like an ominous warning than a gesture of good faith. I shiver as the driver ushers me into the back seat, taking care to ensure that my dress doesn't get caught in the door.

A ten-minute drive later, we arrive before an exclusive venue on the outskirts of Mayfield. Blake didn't pick just any event to stage his apparent innocence. He chose the Hollings-sponsored benefit gala—an event that once was the mainstay of our societal events. It blows my mind that I forgot about it in all the chaos.

Despite—or perhaps because of—the rumors swirling around its newest board president, reporters are out in droves tonight, positioned near the entrance of the ballroom behind metal barricades. The moment I step from the car, a frenzy of flashing cameras and shouted questions ensues.

Apparently, my date decided against meeting me at the door tonight. So I enter alone, using one hand to maneuver the skirt of my dress while advancing with my head held high. A pair of ushers dressed in tuxedos allow me inside and I join the fray, a fallen princess among a sea of watchful enemies.

My most daunting opponent doesn't use stealth or violence to unnerve me tonight, however. I find him in the foyer, directing guests, his smile gallant. Until he spots me, that is, and his mouth falls into a hard line that takes my breath away.

His narrowed gaze slices through my delicate ensemble like a razor, ripping down to the bone underneath. I can't stop my fingers from self-consciously covering my breasts, and the motion only makes a muscle in his jaw lurch. Two involuntary steps take him away from the pretty woman in a red cocktail dress he'd been directing, and I can tell he intends to turn back, ignore this slight.

But he can't. Not when I've been this fucking brazen.

"I take it that no other option was suitable?" he murmurs, snatching my wrist the moment he's close enough while positioning his body so that no one else can see the possessive motion.

Up close, I sense just how angry he really is. Fury bellows from his nostrils, mingled with every harsh exhale he takes. His fingers twitch against my skin, reminding me of his earlier confession: *I see that girl and I want to crush her.*

"Tell me I look beautiful," I command him, my voice weak. Beautiful even quaking with rage and pain. Beautiful even in another man's wedding dress.

Something chilling alights his features as his mouth cocks into a cruel excuse for a smile. "You always look beautiful," he declares. "Fucking beautiful."

"Now, kiss me." I can't stop my teeth from skewering my lower lip as his attention turns to it. "Make it good, darling. Good enough to convince everyone here that I don't want to strangle you or that you don't want to…" More-than-strangle me. God, the violence promised in his gaze is too horrifying to give voice to. "Think you can manage that?" I settle on daring.

He scoffs. The next second, I'm in his arms, his palm pressed against my lower back, burning me through satin and lace. His mouth claims mine without warning, his teeth gnashing my tongue when no one can see. I jump at the sharp pinch, but he growls in answer, licking at the claimed flesh. I'm gasping as he pulls away and lowers his mouth to my ear.

"And when do I get to rip this fucking dress from your body and show you just how *beautiful* I think you really are?"

I swallow hard and brace my hand against his chest to find enough leverage to back away a single step. "After you make some speech filled with lies about how much I mean to you. How much you care about me. How much—" I suck in a breath. Damn it. My eyes burn, blinking frantically. I force air into my lungs and soldier on. "How much you love me.

Go on. This is my company too. I don't want to see it ruined. But, after this, I've given you everything."

And he couldn't even give me one promise to cling to.

"Snow—" He grips my arm tighter when I try to pull away. "You wait for me," he demands, his tone rough. "I'll know if you don't and I swear I'll come after you and drag you back. You wait for me."

I pull away, breathing rapidly as I delve deeper into the crowd, imagining him hunting every step I take. But when I finally turn to get my bearings, he's gone. I'm alone in a realm of unfamiliar faces all jostling for a look at the woman with bloodshot eyes in a beautiful dress.

"You certainly know how to make an entrance."

I flinch as someone loops their arm around mine. Sloane. She's cutting a stunning figure in a black gown almost as revealing as the one I wore at the auction.

She tugs me confidently through the center of the room, smirking as we draw attention with every head turned. "I didn't think you'd come."

A hitch snuck into her voice. Perhaps I stole her chance at the spotlight once again? I don't have the energy to decipher her motives. Instead, I let her parade me around like a shiny token, unable to avoid my "date" for the evening.

It's like he positions himself to constantly remain in my line of sight though he never once looks my way. He mingles, and laughs, and talks up a room of people who secretly think him to be a predator. As charming as he can be, however, none of them dare say as much to his face. I now understand why he's maintained his precarious spot at the company for so long when any other man would have been driven out for less scandal.

He's Blake Lorenz and the world has no choice but to acknowledge that fact. He spins lies so emphatically that you start to question the visible truth.

"You're distracted tonight," Sloane teases, her breath tinged with her fourth glass of champagne. "Do tell. Do tell."

"Why?" I disentangle my arm from hers, unconvinced by her playful frown. "So that whatever I say can show up in tomorrow's papers?"

She winces. "I'm sorry. Beautiful Snowy, desired by all. I didn't think you'd mind."

Something in her tone draws my attention. Pain? Whatever it is, she dispels it with a charming grin. "Don't be too upset?"

"Why Daniel?" I find myself asking. "I know you... I know—"

"I was never the one he wanted," she says, her gaze fixed somewhere far beyond this room, I suspect.

"What are you saying?"

She stiffens and shakes her head before plastering a fake smile onto her otherwise blank expression. "Nothing. Oh, he looks dangerous."

I follow the line of her gaze, confused by the statement. Oh God. Marching onto a raised dais serving as a makeshift stage, his eyes aglow, Blake Lorenz looks *more* than dangerous.

He looks insane, hunting for me in the crowd as he takes the microphone.

"I'd like to make an announcement," he declares, and it's as if the whole world stops, turns, and waits.

Dread forms a weight around my heart, growing heavier with every second he holds my gaze. So many unspoken words pass between us in this instant, which terrify me when he finally opens his mouth again.

"Thank you all for coming. Especially given current... rumors swirling around myself."

An audible murmur runs through the crowd. Like any manipulative bastard, he knows the best way to capture every ear here—through intrigue and spectacle.

Satisfied by his captive audience, he continues. "With that in mind, I'd like to start off this night by announcing that not only will I be pledging a generous donation to the Haven Project, but I am officially making Hollings Incorporated a designated benefactor of such an amazing charity."

A part of me bristles at how easily he utilized my donation for his own needs. Does the man have no ounce of shame? Or perhaps he does. There's something in his gaze that sends my heart hammering against my chest. Something raw and real, impossible to ignore: guilt. He doesn't hide it from me for once. He lets me in, allowing me closer than I've ever been to the emotions he guards, even while across a spacious ballroom.

"Haven and the ideas it represents mean more to me than a worthy cause," he continues, his voice thick. "Rape, sexual abuse, and assault are the taboo deeds we usually regulate to tabloids of sordid news stories. But you and I know the dirty, dark secret lurking in most homes, even here in Mayfield. The black eye you use makeup to disguise. The bruises we can't explain away. The illicit touches we excuse because it hurts too much to call it what it is…" He looks at me directly and so many words spill into the air between us.

A million secrets.

A hundred memories.

Perhaps a single, earnest apology.

It feels like an eternity passes this way—but in the end, it must be no longer than a few seconds. Clearing his throat, he turns to the crowd still hung on his every word. "It hurts. So you turn your shame and embarrassment into anger, and you direct it at the people who mean the most to you."

I inhale sharply, steeling myself for what he might confess next. His tormented expression claims it's brutal.

"When I… When I was assaulted," he says hoarsely to audible gasps of shock that erupt throughout the room, "I blamed myself. I blamed the people who I thought were supposed to protect me. And I punished them and myself. But now I realize, even after the physical abuse was over, by continuing to hate, I was only destroying myself and continuing to be a victim instead of a survivor. It's organizations like Haven that offer resources to help young boys and girls who felt as powerless and helpless, as I once did, move on from being victims to survivors... Thank you."

He leaves the stage in a rush as my mind spins, a whirlwind of agony. He meant it, every word. I may not know the man he's become, but I knew Brandt. I knew that tortured look in his gaze, lingering just long enough for him to tell his secrets to me. Only me. I remember the nights his father antagonized him the most. And I remember what snippets of his ordeal in prison Blake Lorenz let slip: *Once, they tried to show him what rape was, Snow.*

"Heavy stuff," Sloane murmurs beside me, snapping me back to the present. She downs her last glass of champagne and grabs my arm. "Come. I want to get fresh air." She's in the process of fishing a cell phone from the cleavage of her dress. It's buzzing, and she frowns at the number before stowing the item back in place. "Come."

"But..." My gaze tears from regal figure to figure, hunting for a familiar face.

There. He's fixated on me, slowly pushing his way through the crowd. They part adoringly. By baring his soul, he's won their fickle hearts over. But mine?

"Just five minutes," Sloane pleads, tugging me forward.

I expect her to head for one of the terraces overlooking a courtyard with a bubbling fountain. Instead, she takes a turn down a winding hallway and shoulders a metal door open.

"Where are we?" My nose wrinkles in the blisteringly cold air. Rather than a beautiful, scenic view of one of the venue's gardens, I make out the shape of a dumpster and a white van parked along a narrow alley. It must be a service entrance of some kind.

Giggling, Sloane tugs me forward, forcing me to heft the skirt of my gown with my free hand.

"Where are we going…" Motion catches the corner of my eye. Then pain. *Wham!*

Stars float across my vision. The world tilts violently sideways, and something firm catches my fall. I throw my arms out, a desperate attempt to get my bearings.

Then blackness.

SEVENTEEN

CONSCIOUSNESS RETURNS IN SLOW, painful drips, and only snippets of sound give me context to my surroundings. I'm lying flat, tasting salt. Night air nips at my skin as the faint roars of traffic allude to the fact that I'm outside. Near the gala?

Scuffling footsteps bolster that suspicion. I recognize the distinct click of high heels, echoed by a heavier, steadier set of footfalls.

"What…what are you doing?" a woman demands, her thickening accent betraying her fear. Sloane?

I try turning in her direction, but my limbs won't obey. My head feels too heavy. Agony shoots through my skull, focused around a single, throbbing point. God…was I struck with something?

"You weren't supposed to hurt her! You were just supposed to—"

A sudden crack echoes and the woman goes silent. Alarm doesn't even have the chance to sink into my limbs before a sound like a car engine revs into gear and the world sways beneath me. Someone has my arm in a vise grip, using it like a leash to shove me against a firm surface. I scramble to regain my bearings, running my fingers over an uneven material in a desperate bid to place it. Soft. Rugged. Carpeting?

"Don't move." An unfamiliar touch shocks my cheek.

That voice…

"Not so fast," I'm warned when I attempt to move. Something chafes against my eyelids when I try to open them, obscuring my vision. "If you can hear me, just nod."

Swallowing hard, I do, once.

"Good."

The pressure withdraws, and my heart races as I try to settle on a possible culprit. Ronan? Hunter? Again, I'm sure I know that voice, but my throbbing head fails to come up with a name. Someone gruff, nervous…well-spoken?

"You'll be safe, as long as you do what I say," my captor warns, furthering the mystery.

Licking my lips, I risk his ire to ask, "Who…who are you?"

There's no reply. Silence mingles with the perpetual sirens that wail throughout the city and my fear only grows. We're moving, I realize. Fast. Away from the venue to somewhere unknown. In a car or a van?

"Where are you taking me?" I croak, trying once again to probe for answers.

For the second time, I receive no response. In its absence, my headache worsens, and pain feeds a million dangerous suspicions.

"Someone offered me more, Little Hollings," Lyle Harlow claimed.

Would the man really be so bold?

Suddenly, the world comes to a stop and I'm jostled onto my side. A door opens and cool air tickles my cheek, alerting me to the fact that we're not outside, but somewhere enclosed. A garage? A hand latches onto my shoulder before I can be sure, and I'm shoved upright onto trembling legs.

"Move," I'm commanded. A warning grip on the back of my throat keeps me from resisting the contact as my captor steers me forward. He's panting.

Straining my ears, I strive to notice any detail I can. Silence, mostly. It encases us in an echo chamber of unsteady footsteps and frantic breaths. There's only two of us, a fact my captor seems desperate to disguise. He's moving unsteadily, creating the illusion of a million pattering footsteps.

"Don't fight," he warns, tightening his grip until I nod frantically in agreement. "Keep moving."

We're in a narrower space now, where the air feels even more enclosed. I jump as a door creaks, opening and closing behind us. We're alone, and the figure I'm with towers above me. Their breath heats my shoulder blades, bearing down on my scalp.

"Stop." He shoves against a firm surface before I can comply on my own. "Sit."

I manage to perch myself on what feels like a metal chair without falling. The skirt of my gown bellows out around me, creating a makeshift barrier between me and the man I sense steadily advancing.

"Put your hands behind your back. Please."

And suddenly, it clicks: I know that gallant tone of voice. Even now, he can't resist the suave air of politeness bred into him—a benefit of ten years of finishing school.

"Daniel." My voice rasps, echoing off our surroundings. "Daniel, is that you—"

"Shut up." He doesn't hit me, but his hand lands over my shoulder, imparting a subtle warning. "Do it," he rasps, damn near begging. "Put your arms behind your back, Snowy."

When I do, he takes them both. Something thin is wound around both of my wrists, tethering them together tightly.

"Now, open your mouth."

Terror threatens to shatter the cohesiveness of my thoughts. *Focus, Snow*, I tell myself. *Don't panic...*

"Now!"

My lips part woodenly, allowing something rough to be shoved between them, which prohibits any attempts to speak. Cloth? Sweat lingers in the fabric, betraying that it's an item of clothing. A glove? Tie?

"I'm going to take the blindfold off," my captor says as his footsteps once again move behind me.

Suddenly, the cloth over my eyes is withdrawn, which allows me to make out a darkened room lit only by a dim floor lamp. Dingy carpet and water-stained walls give no clue of my surroundings—somewhere far beyond the glimmer of downtown Mayfield, I suspect.

Somewhere secluded.

"I'll only tell you this once, Snowy," my captor warns, his tone rough, nearly imploring. "I don't want to hurt you." A shadow flickers over the floor, tall and slender. When he finally comes into my line of sight, I'm grateful for the gag stifling my gasp.

In the harsh, artificial lightning, Daniel Ellingston III looks like a stranger—though I suppose he always has been. A few short months have left his once-coifed blond hair wildly overgrown, with lanky strands falling into his bloodshot eyes. His gray suit is crumpled and unkempt. Faint body odor warns that he hasn't washed in a while, either—him, the man who groomed himself better than I did while we dated.

Alarm spurs my faltering heartbeat, stiffening my posture. At a glance, I can tell he's alone. But for how long?

"Don't look at me like that." Groaning, he runs his fingers through his hair, flicking the worst strands away from his face as his lips contort into a shadow of his infamous grin. "Even now, I can't seem to impress you, can I, Snowy?"

Something warns me not to react. I stare ahead blankly, tracking every unsteady step as he paces in a small circle before me. He's holding an object in his right hand, something he absently taps against his thigh. My brain recognizes the shape, but a part of me refuses to put the proper name to it. The Daniel Ellingston I knew would never carry a gun, especially not one formed of stark black metal. It simply didn't mesh with his image.

What could have transpired in nearly three months since his disgrace to push him to this point?

"I can explain everything." He frowns at the weapon before he tucks it behind his back and out of sight. "You just wouldn't understand," he stammers. "That's why I couldn't tell you before."

Tell me what? I do my best to nonverbally convey the question as calmly as I can. Blank expression. Imploring gaze.

Suddenly, he whirls on his heel. "That smug bastard had it all fucking planned, I bet," he growls, still running his free hand along his scalp. "That motherfucker. He turned you against me. How is that for irony? So much for hating the fucking Hollingses—"

No. The thought feels instinctive, like the little voice most people sense before touching a hot stove or running over pavement visibly slick with ice. *Don't. This might hurt. Tread carefully.*

So much for hating the fucking Hollingses…

"You already know." Daniel pauses his manic march and cocks his head, studying me with a shrewd gaze.

The disguise I fought to uphold fails. I can't stop my eyes from lowering to the gun. He's tapping it again, recklessly against his thigh.

Chuckling, he lifts it, his expression puzzled. "That bastard is more dangerous than he looks. I have to, Snowy," he says in a rush. "I have to carry this damn thing now because of him. And you know it. I can see it on your face."

My face: lips flattened; wide, watering eyes; a throat that won't stop swallowing hard, desperate to fight back the emotion threatening to overwhelm me.

"I thought he'd gotten to you," Daniel says with a hollow laugh that chills me to the core. "But he hasn't, has he? You were always too smart for your own good, Snowy. I should have told you from day fucking one."

Told me what? This time, I don't want to know the answer. It's like I can sense it unfurling anyway, in the shadowy recesses of my mind where only the darkest fears dwell.

"I did what I did," Daniel admits, cutting his gaze beyond my head. "It was wrong. I know that—but I would have never gotten the idea if he hadn't... Fuck!" He slams the butt of the gun into his hip, cursing under his breath. "I should have known the bastard had an ulterior motive. You were never supposed to know. It was never supposed to go public."

A sickening sensation creeps through my stomach, threatening to upend everything balanced precariously inside it.

It congeals into a chilling suspicion that haunts my thoughts before Daniel even parts his lips to utter, "That bastard Blake Lorenz. He set me up, Snowy. That bastard took everything from me. And, now, he's stolen you too."

"I SHOULD HAVE KNOWN BETTER than to ever trust that son of a bitch," Daniel snarls, though I barely even hear him. His voice takes on a dream-like quality, like something recalled from a nightmare. Distant and formless.

For a moment, this dark, dingy room fades and all I can see is the beautiful backdrop of my dream penthouse and the man who dwells inside it. His blue eyes meet mine unflinchingly, devoid of a single ounce of shame.

"What did you expect?" I imagine him snarling. "After all, you hurt me first. You betrayed me first. You were stupid enough to fall in love with me all over again..."

"Snowy?"

I flinch as warmth brushes my cheek. Daniel. He's frowning down at his fingers, and at a glance, I see why. The tips are glistening red. Dread lances through my chest as my skull throbs in response. How badly am I injured?

"I didn't mean to hurt you," he says, his voice thick. He reaches for me again, but I can't stop myself from cringing. He stiffens and then lowers his hand with a sigh. "I didn't… But I had to get you away from him. You don't understand!"

So tell me. The words wind up garbled by the gag, but he nods in understanding regardless.

"I can't. I…" He stops pacing, balanced on the tips of his toes like a cornered animal ready to bolt. "What the fuck was that?" His head swivels toward the door as his hand shakily raises the gun.

My heart lurches at how his finger twitches over the trigger, and another indiscernible moan breaks from my throat.

"Shhh," he snaps in annoyance, turning to me once more.

He approaches my chair to stroke the side of my face. Clenching my jaw, I do everything possible not to resist the motion. At the same time, I tug my wrists, testing the strength of the binds: alarmingly tight. Inhaling through my nose, I attempt to meet Daniel's gaze, but his emerald irises are unfocused, darting toward the corners of the room.

Where Blake looks perpetually exhausted, Daniel seems like a zombie, reanimated to react on only the basest human responses.

"I know it was wrong, Snowy," he says. "But I thought… We were supposed to be married when it happened. I would have control of the Hollings Estate and you'd never have to know. I'd keep your brothers on, of course. Everything would be as it was…"

He's rambling and my brain struggles to catch up. *Married. Estate. My brothers.*

All of it leads to one chilling conclusion: Daniel wasn't just a greedy fool caught up in an investigation's web. He planned this. He planned to steal my family's company out from under me all along.

And only one man was devious enough to show him how.

"He came to me six months ago," Daniel says hollowly. "Not that I can fucking prove it. He's a clever, clever son of a bitch. He made it seem like an easy way to consolidate my power in the industry. He'd take a small cut and come on as a primary investor—your brothers jealously guarded their board of directors. Damn… You can't blame me for wanting *some* shred of control. They were so fucking arrogant."

And for a good reason. Almost overnight, Daniel managed to betray the sliver of trust placed in him and wreaked havoc on my family from within.

But he couldn't have done half as much damage alone.

"He said that all he wanted was the company," Daniel continues. "Just a few goddamn shares. He wouldn't humiliate your family in any way. All I had to do was allow him to invest and we would… It doesn't fucking matter!" He shakes his head sternly and refocuses his gaze on me. "It all went to shit, Snowy," he croaks. "Suddenly, the fucking Feds were on my doorstep. Everything was in the papers. You hated me. And that sick son of a bitch. He's dangerous, Snowy. He has a bulldog that he keeps on a leash. Some thug named Harley or Larow—"

Harlow. That name echoes off the inside of my skull in a morbid loop. Harlow. Lyle Harlow. Lyle Harlow.

"It's funny… That was the contact who fed me all the information I needed to make the false investments. And he threatened you, Snowy. Threatened to hurt you if I didn't leave the city—"

Another muffled sound escapes me, garbled by the gag. Even I can't decipher the plaintive howl. Perhaps a simplistic word: no. No, no, *no*. I'm shaking my head before I realize it, blinking back burning beads of moisture that escape down my cheeks in searing rivulets.

Daniel bought my contract with Harlow. But that meant another man had introduced him to my father's old lackey. Another man who knew him prior. Had he known the truth all along? Toying with me. Torturing me for days until I finally broke down and revealed the truth.

Was everything that happened since just another lie? Some sick, twisted way for him to save face? I'd thought him the shattered remnant of the boy I loved, but maybe he was more of a monster than a man all along…

"Listen to me, Snowy," Daniel implores, continuing to speak even as my thoughts drift and dissipate.

I'm far beyond this room, reliving every moment and every word. Every fucking touch and caress. Every lie. They're all poison, building in my veins, choking the breath from my lungs.

"Snowy!"

I blink and find Daniel in front of me, his eyes worriedly scanning my face.

"Stay with me—"

"Get the fuck away from her."

That voice. Like a hook, it sinks into my soul and my entire being swivels toward the sound. Rather than a knight in shining armor, I find a shadowed figure dominating the doorway.

He looks like hell, burning and ruthless. Wind has disrupted his curls as if he ran all the way from the ballroom. But he's unarmed, and I suspect he came alone. Honed like a laser, his gaze finds me and narrows, brimming with rage.

"She's bleeding, you fool," Blake says coldly. "What the fuck did you do—"

"Shut up!"

Blake can't see Daniel's face from his position, but I can. Fear sinks into my muscles, and my wrists flex, testing the give of my binds again, ignoring the pain. Dread ramps up, coaxing a terrifying lullaby out of my heartbeat. *Thump. Thumpthumpthump.*

"Just shut the fuck up—"

"Can you hear me, Snow?" Blake eyes me without flinching, even as the barrel of a gun sways in his direction.

In this moment, I could stomach anything—any ounce of disgust or grudging concern. Anything but this: his eyes practically glowing, fixated on my face, begging for a response. *Can you hear me?*

My chin jerks in acknowledgment and he nearly deflates with relief.

"Good. Listen to me, Snow. Everything's going to be all right."

"Don't fucking move!" Daniel has both hands on the gun now, but he can barely steady it enough to point it in Blake's direction. The barrel sways back and forth, dangerously erratic.

"Put the gun down, you fool," Blake snarls. "Before you blow your damn head off—"

"Or yours."

I've never heard Daniel sound so unpolished. So… desperate. He's shaking from head to toe, his skin alarmingly pale—and I realize I was wrong before. He's *terrified*. Riling him up now is the wrong course of action to take—even Blake seems to realize that.

He raises his hands in a gesture of surrender, though his posture doesn't betray anything of the sort. "Put the gun down." As he speaks, he inches forward a careful step.

"I said don't move—"

"Daniel," I rasp, or at least I attempt to around my gag. "Please... Don't do this."

"You believe *him*?" He turns to me, his expression stricken. "Do you?" His hand twitches, and the mouth of the gun yawns before me, endless.

"Stop it, you fool." My blood runs cold at the apparent fear cracking that impervious baritone I know so well. For the first time Blake Lorenz sounds terrified. "Lower the fucking gun," he snarls. "Or point it at me. Focus on *me*—"

"Shut up!" Wide, Daniel's gaze darts from me to Blake. "Now, you pretend like you give a damn about her?" he wonders. "Bullshit! Maybe I should just do it, huh?" The gun centers over me again, but this time his hand holds it steady. "Maybe this is the only way you'll fucking feel a shred of guilt. *You* did this—"

"Daniel, please." My wrists are on fire, but I think I have enough leverage to slide one hand free. Just a little more...

"What the hell was that?" A floorboard creaks, drawing Daniel's attention over his shoulder. Suddenly, his back is to me, his movements erratic. "I said don't fucking move!"

Panic urges my body into motion. I wrench at the binds, my eyes watering as agony crawls up either limb. Skin peels and gives way in searing shreds—until, at last, freedom! The sudden shift in motion throws me forward and off the chair.

"No!" Daniel lunges toward me, his aim unsteady. "Stay there—"

"Get the hell away from her!"

Just like that, chaos descends. A heavy force slams into my body, knocking me to the floor, as a monstrous sound tears through my eardrums. The world explodes into a mixture of clamor and noise. I taste blood. Hear church bells, constantly ringing.

Ringing.

Then…silence.

A coppery scent reaches my nostrils as the weight pinning me to the floor suddenly goes limp, rolling off me. Footsteps tear from the room, leaving me alone with the downed figure.

And all I see is blue.

Glazed.

Empty.

Dying blue.

EIGHTEEN

BRANDT NEVER LET me win our games, not even when I begged to. He always made me fight for a victory, but he never played dirty or used underhanded tricks to ensure one. Blake Lorenz, on the other hand, plays unfairly without even trying. Only a true monster would die now, when I hate him so much. When I'd kill him myself for answers.

He *can't* die now.

The thought hammers against the inside of my skull as I race down the hospital wing on trembling legs.

A doctor dressed in white awaits me at the end of the corridor, his face grim as he surveys some documents attached to a clipboard. "He'll need surgery," he says, his tone stern. "Afterward, we'll have a better idea of where to go from there."

He rushes through a set of double doors before I can question him. Alone, all I can do is sit and wait. It feels like hours pass, though in the end, I'm not sure how long it takes for a nurse to finally emerge from the cordoned off area, her mouth slack with exhaustion.

One look at me and she recoils. When I glance down, I see why: my beautiful, white, ridiculous dress is stained with blood. I'm shaking. Dried tears streak my cheeks, containing smeared remnants of makeup.

"M-Ms. Hollings?" Blinking, the nurse regains her composure. "He's in a room now," she says in a rush. "You can see him…if you want." She utters the last three words hesitantly, her gaze on my face.

I'm too tired to tailor my expression, and I can only guess what she finds in it. Terror?

"O-okay," I stammer, lurching to my feet. My heart pounds as I follow her through a maze of winding hallways, and I can't help the pathetic metaphor that comes to mind: I feel like, with every step, I'm traversing the landscape of my soul —or how I imagine it to be, anyway. Clean and white, save for that one realm only he could dominate. It smells like blood and is stained with shadow and stark reality.

The moment I reach the doorway to his room, I realize that once again Blake Lorenz has already foiled my plans. He's standing, a sight that I have to blink twice just to accept. One of his hands clings to an IV pole for balance while the other holds a cell phone to his ear.

"Find her. Please," he demands, his voice rasping and hoarse. "I need to see her. Just find her—" He breaks off abruptly, spotting me in the doorway. Slowly, he lowers the phone, even as the distorted voice of someone blares from the speaker. "Snow," he says, his eyes widening. "You're here."

"Not for long." I don't intend to sound so cold, but I don't try to soften my tone either. He looks awful. A hastily tied hospital gown leaves his backside exposed, baring his scars to the harsh daylight that enhances every brutal imperfection in the flesh. A bandage clings to his shoulder, already seeping droplets of blood in some places. The doctor claimed the bullet missed an artery by mere millimeters, saving him a lethal or crippling blow.

But it's yet another scar added to the damage he already bears.

"You shouldn't be standing," I hear myself croak.

The next second, he's on the bed, eyeing me from behind a fringe of hair. "What did he tell you?"

He doesn't sound angry for once, or suspicious, or defensive. Just so damn tired. I doubt he slept longer than an hour judging from his bloodshot gaze. He's running on mere fumes now, determined to avoid letting his guard down even for a second. "I know you're angry," he says. "Just let me explain."

"Explain?" I parrot the word in a hollow voice I don't even recognize. "Maybe you can explain how you knew Lyle Harlow before you used him to ruin my family's company."

He winces, gritting his teeth. "I…"

"Were you lying all along?" God, it's unfair how my voice carries more pain than his does. His wound is superficial but mine were always soul-deep, impossible to heal. "Why? Just tell me why? Did you enjoy watching me suffer?"

"No!" He forms a fist and slams it into the bed. When I jump, he clears his throat and forces the fingers apart. "No… I came back, needing money. My father's businesses were under attack in Europe."

I say nothing, remembering what he mentioned about Masha's husband.

"Admittedly, I could have taken any company," he adds. "But real estate is my forte and I needed enough collateral to sever my family from his creditor, once and for all."

"So you took over Hollings enterprises," I deduce.

He nods, his expression weary. "More than that. I wanted all of it—but you have to believe me when I tell you that I had nothing against you or your brothers. Not at first. You were cogs in the machine, insignificant in the grand scheme. But then…" He swallows hard, his gaze darkening. "I reached out to Lyle Harlow for assistance. Your father wasn't the only one who utilized his 'talents'—but the bastard saw right through me, I don't know how. He called me out by name, and he mentioned you. How you jumped at Forrest's beck and call, so eager to do his bidding. I spent years believing the worst Snow, but I never hated you. Not like I did then, hearing him describe it. Then seeing you…"

He blinks as if remembering where he is.

"I lost my fucking mind, seeing you again. Healthy. Happy. I'd always imaged you the same shy, awkward little girl, but you weren't. You were living, when I was just a shell of who I used to be. I can't even think of myself as Brandt anymore."

I remember a chilling snippet from the night he took my virginity. *I'm not him,* he swore. *Not anymore...*

"Still, I planned to avoid you. Leave you to Daniel. But then I saw you." He laughs brokenly, shaking his head. "You weren't just living, but you were *thriving*. Perfect, beautiful Snowy Hollings without a care in the world—"

"You sent the book to my engagement gala," I croak. His slow nod compounds the agony ripping through my chest. Of course he did.

"I wanted to see how you'd react," he admits. "I wondered if you'd even fucking remember."

But I did remember.

I could never forget.

"And then you came to me at the offices," he adds. "And again at my private residence. It's like you were haunting me, I couldn't fucking escape." He sounds crazed, a man possessed. "Seeing you again drove me insane, Snow. I can't explain it, and I know that it doesn't excuse what I did. But I was so convinced you deserved it, every fucking bit. Until the letters. Until I heard you say what Forrest did and I realized...I was no better than that son of a bitch." He looks up, meeting my gaze directly. His eyes are more than bloodshot now—they're blazing, welling with emotion that takes my breath away. Regret? Can I trust it?

God, I don't know.

"I'm not asking for forgiveness," he insists. "Not even reconciliation. I just want...I just want us to start over. Not Snowy. Not Brandt. Just two people who made fucked up mistakes. That's all I want."

I should leave, I know I should. At the same time, a part of me recognizes that this may be my only chance to do something. Say something. Hurt him. Kick him. Scream. Anything.

My lips part, but all I can muster in the end is...

"Lie down before you rip your wound back open."

He does, a reluctant frown tugging at his mouth. "Snow—"

"Stop!" It's not enough to refuse him, I have to throw my hands out in front of me, a physical barrier against more lies. "I need you to listen to me, for once."

Warily, he stays, but one of his hands remains outstretched, reaching for me always.

It takes everything I have in me not to grasp for him in return.

"I love you." The confession spills out unbidden, laced with so much pain. I could choke on it, if my lips didn't keep moving, churning out admission after admission. "God, even after all you've done. Even now… I love you so damn much. I do—"

"And I love you." The ferocity of his statement robs my breath, making me sway on my feet. "God, I love you—"

"But we're not *right* for each other." Tears spring, welling beneath my fluttering eyelids. Blinking doesn't keep them at bay—they drip down, painting my cheeks in spite. "We're not. Not anymore."

Beautiful sweet Brandt and foolish, selfish Snowy.

The people we used to be are dead and gone. In their place?

Strangers. Hell, I barely recognize the caricature I've become.

But I'm growing surer of one thing: she doesn't deserve *this*.

"Just tell me what else you've done," I plead. "Just tell me everything."

Uncertainty makes his eyes so goddamn blue. Like an ocean, swirling with years of agony I could only imagine. Pain I'm partly responsible for—no. *Was*. Shaking my head helps to drive that new perspective in: I refuse to keep wallowing in guilt.

We hurt each other.

"Tell me."

"Riley Haverty," he says thickly. "I sent her. I gave her a donation large enough to convince her to approach you."

A pinch in my chest has me seeking out the wall for balance. I can't lie. This deception stings just as much as the others. "Why?"

He looks away, his jaw tight. "You needed to speak to someone. Anyone."

"Because you care so much about me?"

"No." He laughs, shaking his head. "Because I know what it's like, Snow. You wouldn't talk to me. Maybe Riley could reach you. Get you to show your face again. Believe in something again."

In a way he was right—a sick, twisted, degenerate way.

"And now?" I ask. "What am I supposed to believe in?"

"Us," he says simply. He starts to stand only to clutch his chest and remain seated. "We lost each other once. I can't lose you twice. I can't."

"But..." My tongue flicks over my dry lips, desperate for traction. "You already have."

"Don't say that."

He's so beautiful like this that I could almost forget. The pain. The torment. Almost. But, even now, pleading for forgiveness, he guards his secrets too well. I can't tell if he's even truly sincere or just pretending.

The strangest fact of all? I don't feel a shred of guilt for doubting him this time.

"Please," he says, but there's no real energy in his voice. Just a plea so raw it snaps me back ten years into the past. When I was just a girl and he was *just* a boy, and there was no hostility between us. "Hear me out—and I know that you don't owe me a damn thing. Just listen…"

He waits, and I linger near the door, my heart swelling in my chest. Just a few steps forward would carry me beyond his reach. I *will* myself to move.

But I'm frozen.

"I thought I lost you once," he says and his rasping tone sinks into me like a hook, leaving me flailing for freedom. "At the lake. And even then, when all I wanted was to hate you, I couldn't—even thinking for a second that you were really gone…" His voice trails off, leaving me with only memory to fill in the gaps of what he holds back. Me in his arms. Him begging me to live.

You don't get to leave me. Not until I let you go.

"And, it nearly happened again. I almost lost you, and I know that I don't deserve forgiveness. Not this time. But fuck, Snow." He looks up, capturing me in his endless blue stare. I'm enthralled just as I was all those years ago, forever under his spell. "I would give anything to hate you. I would. Because it would be easier than the need I feel. I need you, even when you're gone, you're the only fucking thing that feels real."

But not real enough to change for.

"I'm sorry." Finally, my body remembers how to move.

And I'm already racing down the hall, leaving him there.

Alone.

NINETEEN

ONE MONTH LATER...

"THIS IS YOUR CHANCE, SNOWY," a soothing voice urges. "Now, once and for all, you can tell the truth you've been holding onto for so long."

My mouth opens, but the words won't come.

Not yet.

Ten years later and the truth shouldn't be so hard to say. Like stone, it sticks in my throat, forming a wall more formidable than the one Humpty Dumpty decided to sit on.

But once upon a time, a beautiful boy convinced me that I was stronger than any fall. No matter what, I could always piece myself together again.

And, in his memory, I refuse to remain shattered.

Licking my lips, I close my eyes and I let the words come slowly. "The past few months have been a whirlwind for me.

My family fell into financial trouble. My fiancé was convicted of a federal crime." Charges that would soon include attempted murder and assault. "And living through it all made me realize one glaring reality: I can't move forward if I don't look back. Starting with the fact that ten years ago, my father, Forrest Hollings. He…" My voice trails off, reverberating throughout the room with the aid of a microphone. Slowly, I open my eyes again, taking in the multiple onlookers giving me their sole attention. Seated across from me is Riley Haverty, her face schooled into the perfect, caring mask of a talented talk show host.

I have to give her credit. She did seem remorseful for her part in Blake's deception. This moment is my payment. My one chance to speak on *my* terms in my own words.

Does it matter that the whole world is watching?

Maybe not. Beyond the stage lights and the rapt crowd are my brothers, lurking in the shadows. Some parts of my story I won't reveal today—I can't. But one day, when it's right, I'll tell them the rest.

As for now?

Breathing deeply, I turn my gaze to the nearest camera and clear my throat, ripping down the wall I've let silence me for so damn long.

"My father, Forrest Hollings, made me lie," I say, my voice growing stronger with each word. "He urged me to commit perjury. And…when I was just a child…he assaulted me."

* * *

HEALING ISN'T ALWAYS CATHARTIC. Not at first—and especially when your wounds have scabbed over and healed in hideous, jagged scars like mine.

Purging myself of that pain means ripping myself all over again and carefully stitching up the torn pieces.

It hurts like hell, but this time I can survive.

I know I can.

Even if I have to face each battle alone.

"Good morning, Ms. Hollings." I look up as I pass the security booth where a smiling guard greets me with a nod.

Apparently this visit is more welcome than the day I first attempted to meet Blake Lorenz.

It's funny how time can change your perspective so much. Back then I was terrified.

And now?

I'm resigned. In my hand is a simple invitation—more like a summons. Barely a week after my interview went live and Blake Lorenz chooses now of all times to restate his hold over my life.

Like hell.

Today, I refuse to cower. Reassessing my feelings, one word I don't expect lingers on the edges of my mind anyway.

Tentatively, I toy with it, testing it silently over my tongue. *Free.*

Entering an elevator, I find myself swaying on my feet. It's as if a million pounds have been lifted from my shoulders, but as light as I feel, there's an unnerving sense of weightlessness.

One wrong move and I might pitch too far. Trip. Crash.

Or fly.

When I arrive at the top floor, the executive suite is surprisingly empty. The secretary is gone from her usual spot, as is the security guard who usually monitors the property. There are no other employees scurrying about like they did down below.

Save for a lone figure who blocks my path.

His voice reaches me before my eyes finish taking him in. "Snow…"

God, he still looks beautiful. Untouchable, even despite the stiff way he holds his right arm. His hair has grown longer in a few short weeks and his chin is covered in overgrown stubble. As sharp as ever, his eyes fixate on mine, a pulsing, endless blue. "You look…" His lips part before closing again. Then he shakes his head and sighs. "Am I allowed to say that you look beautiful?"

I should refuse him. Run. Leave. My eyes dart to the nearest doorway, a tempting exit.

"Please, Snow." He's closer, advancing a dangerous step. "Please. I just want—"

"What?" I ask, my chin jutting in the air. "To manipulate me again?"

"No…" He frowns and my stomach clenches. "I want to start over."

"So that's why you brought me here?" I keep my chin tilted defiantly, forcing myself to hold his gaze.

"I brought you here?" he says, his brows furrowing. "But *you* invited me here—"

"No. I did."

We turn in unison to find a slender, feminine figure dominating the doorway of the presidential suite. Her blond hair hangs loosely over her shoulders, framing her face and the determined expression on it.

"Masha?" Blake rushes to meet her. "What are you doing here? When did you get back?"

"This morning," she says, enduring his hug. "I wanted to beat the news reports."

"Reports?" Blake turns her to face him. "What reports."

"That we're freed from the debt our father owed," she says softly. "All of it. Forgiven."

"That's impossible." Blake shakes his head. "How?"

"It was simple in the end." Masha looks at me, her eyes blazing. "I played his game. I saw your interview, Snowy," she says, her tone soft. "And to prevent me from giving one of my own, I ensured that we will never have to worry about him again."

"Hanz?" Blake grabs his sister's shoulders, his knuckles white. "You met him? Alone? Are you insane?" His eyes blaze, jaw clenched. But the longer he meets his sister's fearless stare, the more his tense posture deflates.

"We're free," Masha says. Her fingers graze his cheek in a silent caress. "All of us."

She gingerly steps from her brother's embrace, as lithe as a dancer. "I'll meet you at home, Blake. Goodbye, Snowy." With one last nod in my direction, she drifts through the suite, fading into an elevator.

Stunned in her wake, Blake recovers first.

"I swear I didn't lure you here—"

"I guess this means you don't need Hollings Enterprises," I say tightly.

Needling him should be the last thing on my mind. But freedom doesn't shroud me as easily as it does Masha. I still feel the pain underneath it all, biting deeper as he shakes his head, chuckling.

"I guess not," he says, still laughing. "But I still want it—"

"Keep it." Turning on my heel, I start down the hall.

"With *you*." Heavy footsteps advance on my position. Only now do I realize that I've frozen mid-step. Warmth alludes to a body approaching mine, proceeding the fingers that trace my shoulder. "I want to run this company with you, Snow. Together. No games. No tricks."

My breath catches, betraying the weakness I know he can sense. Hope. "How can I trust you?"

There's silence for so long that I assume it's my answer: I can't.

"Wait." His hands encircle my waist before I can even take a step forward. "You won't trust me," he says, his throat rasping. "Not right away. Maybe never, not fully. And I can't lie. A part of me wants to ensure you will, any way I can. Even if I have to lie, or cheat or steal from you to do it. But that's not what I want."

"What do you want?"

"*This.*" His arms tighten around me. "Holding you. Touching you. Knowing that every second of contact is only because you want it to last. I'm on your terms, Snow."

My terms.

"And if I told you to leave me alone from here on out?"

He stiffens. Then gradually his touch withdraws and he paces away. "Then I'll do it. Even if it fucking kills me—but you'd have to say the words."

And he doesn't want me to.

"I don't know if we can ever go back to where we were before," I admit, hating how much that statement stings. "I don't…"

"But we can start over." He's close again. His mouth finds my jawline, his nostrils flaring, taking me deep. "Together. We can start over *together*."

"And how would we cement this deal?" I wonder, tilting my face toward him. "With another contract?"

"We could." His eyes gleam a dangerous hue of blue. "Though I'd prefer something a little more old-fashioned." His gaze fixates on my lips.

"Like what?" I force myself to ask.

He takes his time leaning in, giving me every chance to back out before our mouths connect. Just once. Against my lips, he murmurs, "We can seal it with a kiss."

DO YOU LIKE TWISTED HEROES?

Check out Mischa in XV and Maxim in Obey!

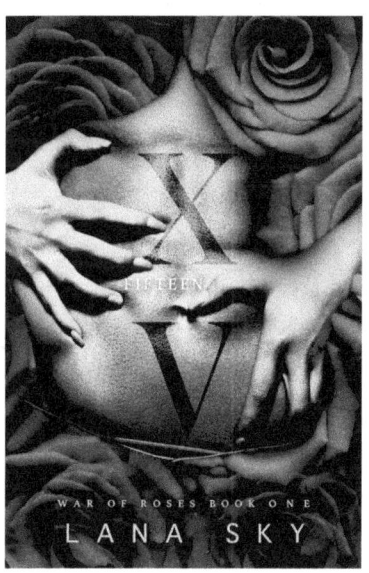

Mischa grates out something that isn't English, capturing my nipple between his thumb and his forefinger, guiding it to a stiff point. Then even words cease to matter. Our language becomes a series of groans and gasps smothered into silk and skin. His fingers roam without care or reason, fanning over my rib cage, plunging through my hair, and grasping strands so hard that my eyes water.

"Look at me." His teeth find my earlobe, grinding it between them. "Fuck. *Look at me*."

I do. And the sight of his face, hard with determination, steals my breath away.

He looks too powerful. Too real. Too raw, hungry for me.

He crushes me with his last thrust, refusing to shift his weight even as he empties himself into me. I'm trapped beneath him, forced to bear every lethal pound. It's almost as if he's trying to drive Robert out through his presence alone.

I try to hang on to that familiar monster. I try…

But, with every passing second, his evil is harder to grasp, like smoke chased away by a raging inferno.

And, without his protection, I'm devoured whole.

Read XV now!

"I've given you enough for tonight," he tells me, sliding his fingers free, ripping away my only lifeline to sanity.

My thoughts cloud over. Can't think. I'm forbidden to move—but my hand jumps anyway, the fingers grasping at the air.

"You want more?" His voice… I've never heard it so thick. It's like he's breaking every word off of stone—hammering humanity out of the monster he really is. "Say it, then. You want more." He snaps his fingers, shining, bloody. "Beg."

I don't want more. I shake my head, biting my lower lip.

He steps back, starts to turn.

I whimper. It's the only sound I can make. Not words. I can't say it.

"Do you want it?" He steps forward, bracing one knee on the cushions of the couch beside me. His fingers come to circle my throat, tilting my head back so that I'm forced to stare into those swirling black holes he has for eyes. "How badly do you want to come?" His fingers sweep down, catching a swollen, bitten nipple between them. "Do you need it?"

Fire licks through my veins, but it's nowhere near strong enough. Harsh enough. I *need* more.

"Y-yes."

When he bears down, I can't hide the scream that rips from my throat. It's too soft. Too damn close to a moan.

"Then fucking ask for it—"

"P-please."

His eyes disappear, narrowed into slits. The next second, he's on his knees, his hands on my hips, dragging me forward. His mouth catches me.

And my body does the screaming for me. It explodes. Ignites. Blows up.

Kaboom! It's a scramble to reassemble myself in the chaos. Nothing in the world compares to his tongue. It's soft. Strong. Licking. Sucking. Breaking. Breaking. Breaking.

This time, I don't get just a taste of clarity. I get a full fucking dose. My thoughts go so clear that, for the first time in my life, I don't feel anything. No fear. No pressure. No stress.

Just *nothing*.

Read Submit now!

A WORD FROM THE AUTHOR

Hey there!

Thank you so much for reading! If you enjoyed the story, please leave a review and recommend the book to any friend you think would love this twisted world. You'd have my eternal gratitude. Even a short sentence goes a long way!

Then, come join the rest of us dark romance lovers in my Facebook Group where you can get snippets, sneak peeks of upcoming books and even help vote on aspects of future novels.

Come to the dark side:
https://www.facebook.com/groups/lanasbeautifulmonsters/

WANT MORE STUFF TO READ?
Join my newsletter and get a **free book**! Plus, you get to stay updated with any new releases, random giveaways and exclusive sneak peeks!
https://www.lanaskybooks.com/newsletter

Other Novels: https://lanaskybooks.com/

FREE BOOK - JOIN MY NEWSLETTER

Dark, Twisted Romance

Join my newsletter and get a **free book**! Plus, you get to stay updated with any new releases, random giveaways and exclusive sneak peeks!

https://www.lanaskybooks.com/newsletter

ABOUT THE AUTHOR

Lana Sky is a reclusive writer in the United States who spends most of her time daydreaming about complex male characters and parenting her Cockapoo Joey. She writes dark, twisted romance across several genres. Her titles include everything from mafia romance to vampires.

facebook.com/AuthorLanaSky

twitter.com/lanasky101

amazon.com/author/lanasky

pinterest.com/lanasky101

goodreads.com/lanasky

instagram.com/lanasky101

bookbub.com/authors/lana-sky

ALSO BY LANA SKY

For more titles by Lana Sky, please visit:

https://www.lanaskybooks.com